60, 90 & U

SAGA OF THE REPTILE KING

Praavin Iyer

ISBN 978-93-5883-041-5

Published in India 2023 by Pencil

A brand of
One Point Six Technologies Pvt. Ltd.
Unit no. 26, Ground Floor, Building A1,
Wadala Truck Terminal Road,
Near Post Office, Antop Hill, Mumbai - 400037
E connect@thepencilapp.com
W www.thepencilapp.com

Author biography

My name is Pravin Iyer, and this is my first effort to create a book as a newcomer to the book market. Since I've worked in sales for so long, I've had a lot of thoughts racing through my head that I'd like to compare to daydreaming. Whenever I saw a situation, I would imagine what would have happened if things had gone this way or that way. I decided to create a book today after meeting many individuals over the course of many years, and I hope you will enjoy it.

CONTENTS

chapter 1 11

chapter 2 31

chapter 3 46

chapter 4 65

chapter 5 85

chapter 6 109

Epigraph

"It's become common practice to kick off every literary work with a quote."
 "Expectation: If we closely observe, we can see the expectations of both a leopard and a pack of jackals. It is the same; both wanted the carcass. But none got it, and in the end, all the fighting was in vain..."

-60, 90 & U by Praavin Iyer

Foreword

Vanlo Marlobus is captured by the Reptile King. Vanlo was a humble, simple, and hardworking farmer. However, despite his hard work, he struggled to make the ends meet. Vanlo narrates his journey up the Red Mountains in search of a grey-green eyed young forest girl. The Reptile king named Kaiman who mixed his soul into the heart of the sea, from the depth of the evil call. From the outer universe to the central and inner deepest crests of the sea, he comes across scenes of brutality, torture, slavery, and horror. What happens when Vanlo finally meets Kaiman? A journey not only into the depths of the Red Mountains jungles but also into the dark recesses of the human soul, The Reptile King? Heart of Darkness is a critical exploration of the spine-chilling truths and hypocrisy of the wizard who told them. Vanlo's epic journey has undergone several twists and turns, from the sea bed to the mountain top. The quest for power has just begun and the sight of how it overtakes the lives of many…..

-60, 90 & U by Praavin Iyer

Preface

Vanlo Marlobus, in the perfect land where a soul paid a humongous price. As he was weakened by his thoughts, a tribal war that shocked the lives of many who took its toll. The damage was deeply rooted in the valley of power seekers. The Reptile King imposes his rule on the defeated. He traded their bodies and souls for his own greed for power. Money is sucked out, they fight each other for the cry of the universal power game to lead them out as the supreme. The Reptile King dint pay any heed to their thoughts. They tried to break a half-white, half-red stone of power. The Reptile King was called Kaiman. He stands alone against the universe for his own law. He is lost into darkness and chaos. Will he rise above the earth? Or, Will his quest make him sail through his struggle? Will he win the demon lord who is enclosed in the box of the wizard's spell? Or, Will he fulfil the destiny of evil? Begin an epic journey of 60, 90, and U the trilogy....

-60, 90 & U by Praavin Iyer

Acknowledgements

I don't know for whom I wrote this story, but when I began writing it I had not realized that writing would be so difficult. When I got going with it I do not know how quickly it grew, and I ended up writing 2 books. So now I present to you the first part of the trilogy. Nearly everything I have is in it, and it is not full. Pain and excitement are in it, feeling good or bad. To my daughter Trisha and my wife Lalitha without whose never-failing sympathy and encouragement this book would have been never finished and stayed low in my memory lane for ever! I take up my pen this year by the grace of Sai baba, and travel back into time.

God and my Guru thank you for making me this capable and helping me complete this book. Without your blessings this would have been impossible.

There are many more people I could thank, but time, space, and modesty compel me to stop here.

-60, 90 & U by Praavin Iyer

Introduction

This epic sea & mountain voyage of Vanlo Marlobus with the entangled soul of The Reptile King, a great half red and half white stone, widely considered one of the greatest power left behind by the great wizards,
"It was the best of times, it was the worst of times, it was the age of wisdom, it was the age of foolishness, it was the epoch of belief, it was the epoch of incredulity, it was the harbinger of light, it was the harbinger of darkness, it was the spring of hope, it was the winter of despair."
The Reptile King, was born with the power of the red mountain thereby enabling him to rule the upper, lower and the bottom world. When The Reptile King stepped out into the bright sunlight from the darkness, the true love story of a man was rewritten by the evil Reptile King for his own selfish greed. How time changes and good makes it's way into the dark knowingly or unknowingly trapped for the life till he/she find the next successor for him/her to be free to die. "The epic journey of Vanlo and The Reptile King reveals the inner urge of power, greed, lust and ME"

-60, 90 & U by Praavin Iyer

chapter 1

The Catch Of The Eye

Once upon a time, Vanlo Marlobus lived on a farm. Every morning, he would travel to his farm and work there. He was a very hardworking farmer. However, despite his hard work, Vanlo struggled to make the ends meet.

 He knew that he needed to come up with a new plan if he wanted to save his farm and provide food to his family. So, he began to research new farming techniques and ways to increase his crop yields.

With determination and perseverance, Vanlo was able to turn his farm around and become a successful farmer.

Vanlo cut quickly and efficiently, slicing through the thick, hard mud with his sharp blades. The crops were very long. He did not need to stretch.

He stopped and looked at the calm weather. Just a little while ago, the wind had been howling through this part of the land. Unseasonal rain had lashed the area. Vanlo ran and stood under a thick canopy of trees to save himself from the rain.

The winds had been so loud that it had been almost impossible to see anything with the naked eye.

And suddenly, calmness had descended, the rain and winds had vanished. They quickly headed to a patch of land with an abundance of water.

The entire purpose of the excursion was to find a way to remove the water. The group knew they had to act fast to remove the water before it caused any damage to the area.

They scouted the area for any possible solutions and came up with a plan to create drainage channels to direct the water away from the woods.

With everyone working together, they were able to successfully remove the water and prevent any potential harm to the ecosystem. As they left, they were grateful for the calmness that allowed them to complete their job.

Vanlo heard a loud yet surprisingly gentle voice. 'Come, I don't want to. It's better if-'

The voice stopped mid-sentence. It would never be heard again. For the wind buried in the voice that had been its source.

Vanlo was left in shock and uncertainty, wondering who the voice belonged to and what they were trying to say.

The sudden interruption and subsequent silence had added only mystery and intrigue to his thoughts.

He may have felt a sense of loss or regret for not being able to hear the rest of the message, but ultimately had to accept that it was lost to the wind forever.

Vanlo turned around. The wetness had made it hard to cut through the muddy land and walk. Under these circumstances, he thought that he had done a good job.

He was now looking away. And then, down at his own feet, a smaller pile of mud blocked his leg. He smiled sheepishly. 'That's more than enough. Let's go back.'

It was clear that Vanlo was tired and ready to call it a day. The muddy terrain had proven to be a challenge, but he was satisfied with the progress he had made.

It was time to head back and rest up for the next day.

He started walking along the river, which had been racing through the forest of Andak. There was a girl on the other side of the farm, and she was deeply attracted to Vanlo.　　`

 It seemed as though the river was the only thing separating them, and Vanlo couldn't help but feel drawn to her as well. As he walked, he couldn't shake the feeling that they were meant to be together, and he made a promise to himself to find a way to cross the river and meet her.

The rushing water may have been a barrier, but Vanlo was determined to overcome it and see where his attraction would lead.

 The girl then started looking at Vanlo, across from a small tree. She was drawn to his smile and mesmerising blue eyes.

'I don't think I have ever seen anyone with such beautiful eyes!' She thought to herself. As she continued to stare, she couldn't help but feel a flutter in her chest. It was then that she realized that she was starting to develop feelings for Vanlo.

She quickly looked away, feeling embarrassed and unsure of what to do next. But deep down, she knew that she wanted to get to know him better and see where this could lead.

From that moment on, Vanlo was on her mind constantly. She found herself daydreaming about him and wondering if he felt the same way. She knew that she had to take a chance and talk to him, even if it meant risking rejection.

The thought of never knowing what could have been was too much to bear. So she mustered up the courage to approach him and strike up a conversation. Little did she know that this would be the beginning of a beautiful love story.

She could not notice anything else nearby. She stared directly into his eyes from afar. Within seconds of gazing into her eyes, Vanlo heard two loud bangs and felt incredible heat from the left side above the ear.

Standing motionless, it was as if he could see life going by. His eyes closed for a while. Within what seemed like a few moments, he saw two love birds fly away. One of them had brushed its body against Vanlo's ear.

Vanlo stood still, lost in thought, as he watched the lovebirds fly away.

The gentle touch of the bird against his ear brought him back to the present moment. He opened his eyes, feeling a sense of peace and contentment.

It was as if the birds had reminded him to appreciate the beauty of life and the small moments that make it so special. Vanlo took a deep breath and continued on his journey, feeling grateful for the brief encounter with the lovebirds.

He had such a look of compassion in his eyes. She ran away in the thick wooded forest; he would have known her, but she disappeared in the forest. It seemed as though she was in a hurry to get away from him, but he couldn't understand why.

He stood there for a moment, staring off into the trees, before finally turning and walking back in the direction he had come from. As he walked, he couldn't shake the feeling that something was off.

He wondered if he should go after her but decided against it.

Whatever her reasons for running away, they were her own. He hoped that she would be okay, wherever she went.

But, being neither a girl of his village nor of the old barrage village, he knew only that here was a girl different from the silken ladies who had ascended from the woods.

He felt drawn to her, curious about her story, and eager to learn more about her.

He wondered if she would be willing to share her experiences with him and show him a different perspective on life.

Despite the social barriers that separated them, he couldn't shake the feeling that they were meant to be.

Here was an air almost of frank boyishness, a smile of pleasant friendliness, and just enough flushing cheek to show womanliness and warm blood.

Overall, who exudes a combination of youthful energy and feminine charm.

Their smile and friendly demeanour suggest an approachable and likeable personality. The slight blush on their cheeks adds a touch of vulnerability and softness, making them even more attractive.

Overall, the user's input describes a person who exudes a charming combination of youthful energy and feminine grace. The individual's friendly demeanour is accentuated by a warm smile and a hint of blushing cheeks, which add to their approachability and likability.

Even her dress was different. It was simple, almost to the point of plainness. Its charm lay in its glimmering sheen, like the inside of a shell. Its draperies were caught up to show slender feet. Overall, a dress that is simple yet charming, with a subtle shimmer and a flattering cut that shows off the wearer's feet, stands out as unique and different from others.

Held closely to the waves of thick, fair hair. Her eyes were like the sea in a storm—deep grey with a glint of green. Things did not come to him at once. He was to observe them as she made her way through the forest.

He watched as she gracefully stepped over fallen logs and dodged low-hanging branches, her dress flowing behind her like a soft breeze. The forest seemed to come alive around her, with the birds singing a sweeter tune and the leaves rustling with a gentler touch.

 As she disappeared into the distance, he realized that the dress was not the only thing that made her stand out. It was her aura and her presence that left a lasting impression on him. He knew that he had just witnessed something special, something that would stay with him for a long time to come.

Her sight was lost as she made an abrupt turn, but, feeling his way, he wanted to follow her. He stopped himself to say, 'I must be sure no one is here. Should I wait until I see?'

Suddenly, she came back to announce that the coast was clear. He halted on the threshold of that inner voice.

The whole air around and below seemed filled with rosy effulgence; this was the heart of the rose. He couldn't help but feel drawn to her, like a moth to a flame. Her energy was infectious, and he found himself wanting to be near her, to bask in her glow.

 As they walked together, he could not help but notice how her every movement seemed to be in perfect harmony with the universe. It was as if she was dancing to a song that only she could hear, and he was entranced by the beauty of it all.

He knew that this chance encounter was something he would never forget, and he was grateful for the opportunity to have experienced it.

Two small white birds were side by side in an alcove. Their covers were pink overlaid with lace and the chintz of the big couch and water reflected the same enchanting hue.

However, there was the freshness of simplicity. She gave him a startled glance.

'Why did she look at me that way?' He kept thinking. Not that he didn't like it. In fact, he found her innocent beauty captivating. As he watched the birds flutter about in their cosy little home, he couldn't help but feel a sense of peace wash over him.

It was as if all his worries and fears had melted away in the presence of these delicate creatures. He wondered how something so small and fragile could have such a profound effect on him.

It was a moment he would always cherish, a moment that reminded him of the beauty and simplicity of life.

Lonely and longing for a haven after the storms that had beaten him, what better could he find than this?

The birds' chirping and fluttering filled him with a sense of joy he hadn't felt in a long time. He realized that sometimes the most profound things in life are the simplest.

As he sat there, watching the birds, he made a promise to himself to find more moments like this, to appreciate the small things, and to live in the present.

He knew that life was unpredictable and that he couldn't control everything, but he could control his perspective and his attitude towards it. With a newfound sense of gratitude and contentment,

Again, he saw a question in her eyes, but this time he did not answer it. She turned and went into the forest, drawing back the curtains of the deep, thick trees.

With a last flashing glance, she was gone, and as he groped his way down through the darkness, it came to him as an amazing revelation that she had taken his coming as a thing to be thankful for, and it had been so many years since anyone had tried entering the forest.

In spite of the fact that she seemed to like Vanlo, a white-winged angel, she was a beauty. It was Constance who was the "pretty one," and tonight as she stood there, gazing up at the stars, she was more than pretty. She was breath taking.

He couldn't help but feel a pang of jealousy towards her, but he quickly pushed the thought aside. He didn't want to ruin this moment by dwelling on negative emotions.

Instead, he focused on the beauty of the night sky and the peacefulness of the forest. He took a deep breath and closed his eyes, feeling this moment of clarity and contentment. As he opened his eyes, he saw a shooting star streak across the sky, and he couldn't help but smile. Life was unpredictable, but in this moment, everything felt perfect.

Her tender face was illumined with an inner radiance. She was younger but more slender, and her colouring was more strongly emphasised. Her eyes were blue, and her hair was gold, as against the grey-green.

She seemed surrounded, by a sort of feminine aura, so that one knew at a glance that here was a woman who would love herself and her lover, who would lean upon protection, and who would suffer from neglect.

These things could not be said at once. In spite of her simplicity and frankness, there was about her a baffling atmosphere. He couldn't help but feel drawn to her, intrigued by the mystery that surrounded her.

He wondered what her story was, what experiences had shaped her into the woman she was today.

But in that moment, as they both gazed up at the shooting star, he knew that it didn't matter. All that mattered was the present moment, the beauty of the night sky, and the connection he felt with this enigmatic woman beside him. Life was unpredictable, but he was grateful for this.

She was like a still pool with the depths as yet unseen, an uncharted sea—with its mystery of an undiscovered world. Now Vanlo was really wondering what was to be done next. He knew going into the forest was not a good thing, as for a long time it was forbidden.

There was a saying that there was a group of animals awaiting humans. If anyone at all entered, they would hunt them down and eat them. The forest was cursed, and strange things happened, so no one from the village was allowed.

Vanlo couldn't shake the feeling that he needed to explore the forest with this woman, despite the warnings and superstitions. He wondered if she felt the same way.

As they gazed up at the stars, he knew that whatever they decided to do, he was contented for this moment and the connection they shared. Life was unpredictable, but he was ready to take a chance and see where it led them.

Vanlo would now work on his farm every day and wait to see if she returned. One day, it so happened that Vanlo had washed his hands and was on his way to the earnest tree to have his lunch.

Before he would bow down to sit, an arrow whisked from his side hit the tree. Vanlo was pushed down by the hit.

He looked up and saw a cloth filled with something carried with the arrow, which hit his shoulder, and he was pushed down. He looked around but found nothing. With fear within him, he tried opening the cloth bundle. There were fresh fruits. Which were only found in the forest. He then looked around again. Nothing is on site.

Vanlo knew he had to act fast. He gathered the fruits and started to run towards the forest, hoping to find her. As he ran, he couldn't shake off the feeling of being watched.

He knew he was not alone with her. The clouds seemed to be closing in on him, and the darkness was getting thicker. Vanlo's heart was pounding in his chest, and he could feel the sweat running down his face.

 He knew he had to find a way out before it was too late. He did not find her in the forest, but he kept searching, determined to not give up until he found her.

The thought of her being in danger fuelled his determination, and he pushed himself to keep going. As he continued his search, he couldn't help but wonder who or what was watching him. Nevertheless, he remained focused on finding her and bringing her back to safety.

Vanlo knew that time was running out, but he refused to give up hope. He would find her, no matter what it took. But of no use; he could not enter the forest, so after being heartbroken that he would not see her he wandered to his favourite place near the lake.

He just loved the view; he could sit here for hours observing the ducks swimming in the lake and the birds flying over and waiting for her to show up.

He was lost in his thoughts when he heard someone coming.

There she was, hiding behind a tree. She was in awe of him. His virility and strength were such that women were ready to fall at his feet.

 Vanlo was watching her, waiting to make a move. She slowed down and pulled a little branch down. He jumped up and ran towards her. She looked in his direction just before he could start running towards her, and in fear, knowing that this was going to be a bad thing, she just vanished.

He stopped by a small pond, partially overgrown with reeds and low bushes. The surface of the pond reflected the sky and rare clouds. It was a summer afternoon. The sun was at its zenith.

Grasshoppers chirped in the grass. Huge dragonflies circled over its surface, looking for their prey.

Vanlo sat down at the edge of the pond. He mentally imagined that this was on a horse, which was now drinking water and eating grass next to him. These thoughts made him not so lonely; after all, his faith was next to him.

Vanlo shook his head. 'No, not yet. That's what's made it so difficult to track her down. She was hidden among the thick forest, raised as one. She probably thinks that she is the one.' he said, laughing.

'In the morning, first I have to follow her around and get to know her. Then, when I find an opportunity, I'll talk to her. See if she likes me or not.'

'Well, I'll go from the other side there, and I'll figure out a good plan. You have to be careful Vanlo; the stakes are high. Very high.' Vanlo did not think anymore; he turned and left.

Vanlo imagined that this was not an easy thing, but a real, big horse was required to ride around the forest in search of her. He was walking with this thought. Vanlo had never ridden along a forest path before.

He started thinking it was hard to believe the girl he was looking at least might have been one from his village only. She didn't look like any kind of threat to anyone.

She had no makeup, and her hair was in a ponytail that looked as though she'd pulled it back in with no mirrors. Her clothes were so plain, too. She was just standing there with her nose in that tree, oblivious to everything going on around her.

Vanlo is hoping to be able to strike up a quick conversation with her. But she was going to be tough to talk to. If she wasn't in the forest, then she was walking down the hills, somehow managing to not run into the deep forest. She had to have ghost senses to pull that off. Vanlo, rolling his eyes, asked, 'What do you want?'

'Why haven't I been able to see you yet? Oh, relax,' he said to himself. 'I found her but haven't had the chance to talk with her yet. I'm where she comes, waiting for her to come. She looked at me as though I'd lost my mind. I was trying to provoke any kind of memory.

I was looking to see if her heart rate would increase, even in the slightest, or if her eyes would dilate. There wasn't any clue indicating whether she was even there or not.

He stood, and suddenly the need to pace overcame him. 'Perhaps I also needed to calm my own nerves.'

No matter how hard he squeezed his eyes shut, that woman's disappearance into the forest remained etched in his memory. He had caught the recognition in her eyes along with her reaction just before all went dark, followed seconds later by the crackle of birds.

He couldn't shake the feeling that there was something he was missing—something important that he couldn't quite put his finger on. He had been waiting here for what felt like hours, but in reality, it had only been a few minutes.

 He wondered if he should call out to her and try to get her attention, but he didn't want to scare her off. He knew that he needed to be patient and wait for her to come to him. But the longer he waited, the more his anxiety grew. He couldn't help but think that he was running out of time.

Much like his previous little adventure outside of the farmland, he thought he should personally investigate it as he had some attachments to it. He returned to the tree and considered her for a moment. 'Does she know me?' He couldn't be sure, but he knew he had to try to find out. He took a deep breath and called out to her, hoping that she would turn around and recognise him.

He waited with bated breath for her response, feeling a mix of anticipation and fear. Would she be friendly or wary? Would she even acknowledge him at all? As he stood there, his mind raced with possibilities, but he remained hopeful that their encounter would be a positive one. Finally, she turned around, and he saw a flicker of recognition in her eyes.

 It was a small gesture, but it gave him the courage to approach her and start a conversation.

'If she knew me a little. There is a difference.' He rubbed tentatively at his own skin. 'I think I will need to get some of that wonderful Ministry issue in the tropics. I fear I may tan.' he winked.

That sudden silence had made him know beyond any question that might ever again arise that there was now a God—God had watched him. It had happened so instantly.

First that great figure in front of him, the sneering laugh, and that last sentence, 'Let her rot. My dear, your chivalry does you credit.'

Then that black, blinding, surging rage and the blow that followed made him not know what he had intended to do. He could not stay now to think of the many things that had led to this climax.

He only knew that as he raised himself again from the body, there was with him no feeling of repentance, no suggestion of fear, only a grim satisfaction that he had struck so hard, and, above all, that lightning certainty that he had had to go.

His brain was entirely alert. He did not doubt, as he stood there, that he would be caught and killed. He himself would not be able to take any steps to prevent such a catastrophe. He was, indeed, acutely interested in his own sensations. Why was it that he felt no fear? Where was the terror that followed, as he had so often heard, upon murder?

Why was it that the dominant feeling in him was that, at last, he had justified his existence? In that furious blow, there had leapt within him the creature that he had always been—the creature subdued, restrained, but always there—through all this civilised existence;

He despised the whole world. He had gone through his life and was now passing through it as a man travels through a forest that has interest and worth for him but that may lead, once it has been traversed, to something of importance and adventure.

He was perfectly friendly to everyone, and it was curious that, with his air of contempt for the wood in general, he had made no enemies.

He wondered at that himself on occasion; the little crooked path soon left the dark wood and merged into the long white road.

 The forest was veiled in mist, but, like a lantern above a stone wall, the sun was red over the lower veils of white that rose from the sodden fields. Some trees started looking like spies along the road. Overhead, where the mists were faint, the sky showed the faintest of pale blues.

The long road rang under Vanlo's step—it would be a frosty night. When the little wood became a black ball in the mist, he was suddenly sick.

He leant against one of the mysterious dark trees and was wretchedly, horribly ill. Slowly, then, the colour came back to his cheeks, his hands were once more steady, and he could see again clearly.

He addressed the strange world around him—the long, flat fields, the hard, white road, the orange sun. 'This is the last time, 'he said aloud, 'the last weakness.'

 He definitely braced himself to face life. There would not be much of it—tomorrow he would be killed; meanwhile, there should be no more of these illusions.

 There was, for instance, the illusion that something was following him, bounding grotesquely along the hard road.

He knew that again and again he turned his head to see whether anything was there, and the further the little wood was left behind, the closer it was.

He must not allow himself to think these things. He was saved, he hoped, and at any rate,

He had done it; it was a good thing. She was in sight, but it was pleasant to think that she would no longer be worried. Then there was that question about what came next. Now the river appeared, darkly and dimly below the road, the reeds rising spire-like towards the faint blue sky.

That question about where she would be—she had never believed in any kind of luck. The protagonist is struggling with illusions and the fear that something is following him. He tries to push these thoughts aside and focus on the fact that he has saved himself and his loved one.

However, he is still uncertain about what the future holds and where his loved ones will be. Now it was a larger question. There had been that moment after the sun had fallen, a moment of intense silence, and in that moment something had spoken.

It is a fact as sure as concrete, as though he himself could remember words and gestures. There had been something there.

Brushing this for an instant aside, he faced next the question of his fear of death. There was no one to save him.

His mind racing down memory lane, he wanted to send his father a word, saying, 'I have killed a beast—fairly—in the open.' That would be all. Despite his uncertainty about the future and where his love will be, he had a moment of intense silence where something spoke to him.

However, he quickly brushed it aside and focused on his fear of death. With no one to save him, he couldn't shake off the feeling of unease that had been gnawing at him since he had embarked on this journey.

The thought of being alone in the face of danger was terrifying, and he wondered if he was truly ready for whatever lay ahead.

But as he sat there, his mind racing with doubts and fears, he suddenly felt a strange sense of calm wash over him.

It was as though a voice was whispering in his ear, urging him to be brave and face his fears head-on.

 And now, for the first time, the suspicion crossed his mind that perhaps, after all, he might escape—escape at any cost. Here on this desolate road, he had met no living soul; the mists encompassed him, and they had now swallowed the dripping wood and all that it contained.

 It had always been said that he was not supposed to be here, as long as he allowed himself to be with anyone. No one had known in which direction he would take his walk; he had come upon the forest entirely by chance. It might quite naturally be supposed that some tramp had attempted the kill.

To the world at large, could there have been no possible motive? But, for the moment, these thoughts were dismissed. It seemed to him now immaterial whether he lived or died. Life had not hither to been such a wonderful discovery that the making of it had been entirely worthwhile.

But he began dimly to perceive that there were larger, crueller issues before him. He had known since he was a tiny child a story by someone about a knight who rode through the forest. About him was the loneliness. He was hurrying now, although he had not formerly been conscious of it, into the lights, comforts, and noise of the dark.

 And now he could see further. He could see that he must always now, from the consciousness of the thing that he had done, be alone. Vanlo cut quickly and efficiently, slicing through the thick leaf stems with his sharp knife.

The dwarf trees were as tall as he saw them. He did not need to stretch. He stopped and looked back to see if someone or something was there. Then he cast a glance at the sun, a short distance away.

He had cut down perhaps half the number of branches in the short distance he had travelled.

Vanlo looked towards the dense forest line, beyond which lay the huge, deep forest. He expected the women he was searching for would emerge from that direction any moment now.

Instead, a loud scream emanated from the forest. Vanlo cast a quick glance at the other side and then moved rapidly in the direction of the sound.

He came to a standstill as a leopard emerged from the woods, tall, ferocious, and dripping wet. It dragged a struggling deer mercilessly by its jaw.

The jaw had been securely tied. The leopard sat alone on the second high branch of the fourth tree, having just started to fully kill its prey.

It looked like he had remained hungry for a long time; the food was to his liking. It shook its head, its eyes clearly focused. Vanlo stood frozen, watching the leopard devour its prey.

He knew better not to interfere with the natural order of things. Instead, he took a step back and observed the majestic creature in awe, admiring its strength and agility.

The leopard awoke to observe unusual activity in the area. As he stepped out his head from the carcass, he came upon jackals and vultures emerging from a distance and ready to attack.

Having to collect their share, they waited for the leopard, who had gone to an even higher branch. Having stayed awake the previous night, the tired leopard had started to observe unusual activity in and around him.

Leopard's eye turned onto the jackals. It had not escaped his notice that, as usual, every jackal was gaping intently at him.

The weather was calm. Just a little while ago, the wind had been howling through this part of the forest.

Unseasonal rain had lashed the area. Jackals had stood under a thick canopy of trees to save themselves from the rain.

The winds had been so loud that it had been almost impossible for them to walk.

And just as suddenly, calm had descended. The rain and winds had vanished. Jackals, along with their group, had been racing through the forest, leading a small pack.

Due to the wetness on the tree, the carcass fell down, and the leopard also jumped to save its meal. The leopard looked closely. It was an unfair fight.

There were six jackals, weaving in and out, attacking the leopard in perfect coordination. But the brave leopard stood its ground, pushing them back repeatedly.

The aggressors were gradually drawing closer. A jackal hit the leopard with its claws, drawing blood. Suddenly, using the distraction of the leopard with another attack from the left, a jackal struck with lethal effect.

It charged in from the right and bit the leopard's tail brutally. Getting a good hold, the jackal pulled back hard, trying to drag the leopard away.

The leopard squawked frantically. Its voice sounds like a wail. But it held strong. It did not move, pulling back with all its strength.

 The intense battle between the leopard and the jackals continued, with the leopard fighting fiercely to defend itself.

Despite being outnumbered and wounded, the leopard refused to give up and continued to resist the jackals' attacks. The outcome of the fight remained uncertain, but it was clear that the leopard was not going down without a fight.

However, the jackal had strong jaws and a stronger grip. Blood burst forth like a fountain. The jackal let go, spitting parts of its tail as it stepped back.

The leopard was protecting its kill from the pack of jackals. The carcass bundle was covered in mud. The leopard gave the last stronger strike, and the jackals turned tail and scampered into the woods. In the end, the leopard was able to successfully defend its kill and drive off the pack of jackals.

 Despite being outnumbered and wounded, the leopard's fierce determination and strength allowed it to emerge victorious in the intense battle.

Expectation: If we closely observe, we can see the expectations of both the leopard and the pack of jackals. Were the same; both wanted the carcass. But none got it, and in the end, all the fighting was in vain. The carcass was finally mixed in the muddy water, and no one could eat it. The lesson from this is to never keep expectations high for anything, or else the result will hit you hard. And coming out of it or accepting it is difficult. It only gives us pain and nothing else.

chapter 2

A Suspicious Shortcut

Vanlo flashlights were on, but the beams hardly penetrated the thickening fog. Often, they stumbled over rocks and into ruts. The night was raw and damp.

Suddenly, he stopped. 'What's that?' For a second, he stood still, and from the woods came a faint cry. 'He-eelp! Come on!' Vanlo cut into the woods on the right and felt his way through the mist shrouded trees. Low branches cut his face, and once he tripped over a huge oak root.

Again, he heard the thin call for help. 'Where the fog is denser.' Cautiously, he moved forward. Suddenly the cry came more loudly—from right below his feet. Vanlo worked his way down the bank.

At the bottom, he stumbled over something bulky, and there came another moan.

He beamed his light on a prostrate figure.

'My leg,' the man groaned. 'I've been shot.' With extreme care, Vanlo pulled aside the trouser cloth torn by the gunpowder.

'There doesn't seem to be much bleeding now, but there might be more when I move you.' Quickly, he wound his handkerchiefs loosely around the man's thigh to use as a tourniquet if necessary.

As he lifted the moaning figure, he fainted. 'No time to waste; you are pretty weak.' peered around into the blanket of fog. 'Suppose we can't find a hideout?' he asked grimly.

'We must,' the man replied. 'You, man, may die if we don't get shelter. We must get this man to a doctor.' Vanlo said as he finished bandaging the leg.

'The bullet will have to be removed.' The situation seems dire and urgent. The man's weakness and the foggy environment make finding a hideout challenging. However, finding shelter is crucial for the man's survival.

Vanlo, who is bandaging the man's leg, knows that the bullet needs to be removed, and that the man needs medical attention.

Time is of the essence, and they must act quickly to ensure the man's safety. Overall, the situation is critical and requires immediate action.

The man's life is at risk, and finding shelter and medical attention is crucial for his survival. Vanlo is doing what he can to help, but time is running out, and they must act quickly to save the man's life.

The victim groaned, and his eyes fluttered open. 'Why, where am I?' he whispered.

Malkmus quickly explained what had happened. 'Sip this,' Vanlo told the victim, 'and you'll feel a lot better. I'll feed it to you.'

When the stranger had finished, he said in a stronger voice, 'Thank you.' Vanlo and Malkmus looked at the stranger for a mighty good turn. The stranger spoke, 'I wish I could repay you.'

'The most important thing is to get you to a doctor,' said Vanlo and Malkmus. Man asked. 'Is anything wrong?'

Vanlo and Malkmus exchanged a look before Vanlo spoke up.

'Well, you've been shot; the doctor will be able to help you more than we can.' Malkmus added, 'We found you passed out in the alleyway.'

'We're just glad we were able to help.' The stranger nodded, looking slightly confused. 'Shot? How did that happen?' Vanlo and Malkmus exchanged another look, unsure of how much they should reveal to a stranger they had just met.

'Say! Would any of you reply?' The man inquired in a feeble voice. The two identified themselves as Vanlo and Malkmus. 'I plumb forgot about getting shot by that gang,' the man went on, 'but you're the ones I was coming to see.'

'My name is Mike Onlow. I have been asking about you, but they told me you'd probably be off,' he went on. 'I doubted if I would catch up to you at any point, even if I could find your hideout.' Onlow nodded.

'My hideout is pretty hard to get to if you don't know these woods. I stay out quite a bit.' Vanlo said with a quizzical look. 'What do you want to see me about?'

'You'd better not do any more talking till you're stronger.' Vanlo and Malkmus advised. But he had been engaged to track down a gang of criminals in Monya.

'They may be up somewhere in the country around Lukinya. Vanlo is being sought out by someone who wants to talk to him about tracking down a gang of criminals in Monya,

Lukinya,' he went on 'Yep, I know the Lukinya country like the palm of my hand,' he murmured. 'Don't reckon with me, as I can't help you much.' said Malkmus.

But I did run up against a gang. 'Vanlo is willing to help with tracking down the gang of criminals in Monya, despite his weakened state. He has experience with the Lukinya country and has encountered a gang before.'

'Tell us about it.' 'Well,' Onlow began, 'I was partners with them, the red stone gang, and a big redheaded daredevil, Bartson. We were working' in the red mountains, and we sure struck it rich.'

'Gold?' Onlow nodded.

'Real pay dirt—we thought we were fixed for life. By the time the vein petered out, we had three bags of gold, which we found stashed behind a rock.'

'Wow! What happened?'

'The night we were ready to leave our claim, we were jumped by the toughest bunch of crooks in Pepper and his gang. They surrounded us, and we knew we'd never get away with our skins and the gold.'

'How did you finally make it?' Vanlo and Malkmus asked.

'Well, my friend was an ex-pilot, and he had an old, beat-up plane out on the plateau. We'd already put the gold on horseback. While we were ready to move Pepper and his boys around to the front, my friend slipped out back and ran for his crate. The gang spotted him. And chased him. We heard his motor, so we knew he got away okay.'

'The rest of us escaped from there.' Onlow's face became bitter. 'We were supposed to meet him up in Hill and split the gold. But we never saw him or the gold again. The funny part of it is that he was a good partner. I'd have staked my life on knowing we could trust him. But I was wrong.'

'Didn't you ever hear of him afterward or pick up his trail?' questioned Vanlo and Malkmus.

'Nope. Never found hide nor hair of him. After that, I came back and looked for you.'

Onlow asked 'Have you any ideas as to where we might look for the criminals you are after?' 'There are a heap of places he might be in the big country out of Lukinya.' Vanlo and Malkmus were excited by this information.

'Thanks for the tip,' they said to Onlow. 'It's tough luck; you're getting shot tonight. It wouldn't have happened if you hadn't started out to see us. But maybe we can make up for it.'

'Right!' Malkmus said, 'When we're out west, we'll try to find a clue to your missing gold.' 'That's kind of you,' said Onlow. 'But I don't think there's much use. If he really stole that gold, there wouldn't be much left. All the same,' he added, 'if you're willing to try, I'll help you if I can.'

Onlow scratched his head and was thoughtful for a moment. 'I don't know if it'll do any good, but I'll draw you a map. That'll be a starting point, anyhow.' Onlow drew a map for them. 'Here's where the claim was,' he said, marking a ಕ. 'This region was called the Budu Cave Area because of a giant snake face rock that stood all by itself on a cliff.'

'Everybody out there knows Budu Cave,' he added. As they tucked the map in, someone pounded. A sound that would have been inaudible a little while ago with the howling winds.

It was unmistakable now—the menacing creak of a gunshot. A common thing with the group. Many of the more accomplished gangsters used the more expensive guns. But the members used the common variety, made entirely of low quality.

These guns were usually more rigid. And they made a distinct sound when fired. 'Everyone, duck!' screamed Vanlo, dropping the map as they leapt to the ground. Onlow responded not so quickly enough, but the heavier wound on his leg made him trip.

A bullet shot in quickly, slamming into his right shoulder as he fell forward. Before he could react, a second bullet struck his throat. A lucky shot. Vanlo rolled as he fell to the ground and quickly steadied himself behind a rock.

He stayed low, his back against the rock, protected for now. He looked to his right; Malkmus was there in a small group when he looked to his left, and the unfortunate Onlow lay on the ground, drowning rapidly in his own blood. The bullet had exited through the back of his neck. He would soon be dead. Vanlo cursed in anger.

And then realised it was a waste of energy. He began to breathe deeply. Calming his heart down. Paying attention now to Malkmus. He looked around carefully.

Nobody was ahead of them. 'The bullet had come from the other direction, obscured by the rock that protected them'. He knew there had to be at least two to five enemies.

There was no way a single shooter could have shot two bullets in such rapid succession. He asked Malkmus. 'Their anything.' Malkmus told him about finding Onlow with the gunshot wound. Then they improvised a stretcher, and Vanlo and Malkmus carried the injured trapper out to the hole where Malkmus was hiding.

While they were placing him, a few moments later a few more rounds of gunfire were heard. He looked at Malkmus again. He had stopped moving. The jungle was quiet. It was almost impossible to believe that just a few short moments ago, brutal violence had been unleashed.

Farewell, brave Onlow. May your soul find purpose once again? Vanlo and Malkmus caught snatches of commands whispered in the distance. 'Go to... Tell the Lord they are here.' They heard the hurried footsteps of someone rushing away. It was probably just a few miles away now.

At the fare, Vanlo could see the jeep of Onlow standing; he made a signal to Malkmus to go and started the engine, and they took off. 'We have to go to the city,' said Malkmus. 'I have no money for that,' Vanlo said. 'I'll look after that,' said Malkmus. 'No, you won't.' Vanlo said with a smile.

'We'll take the backwater to Bayport. You bet!' Vanlo added. They had drove all night and arrived in Bayport at dawn. 'You look as though you're in need of a good meal.' Malkmus stated to Vanlo. 'We'll fix something right now. Vanlo said he was chasing outlaws! Are we headed for trouble again?'

Malkmus called the nearby friends and told them that we needed a few to travel with us. By the container ship hiding beneath and reaching the city unnoticed.

He then sent a few to the port to check on their plans and report back. 'We have one hour to shower, dress, and drive to the port, and buy our stuff.' They wasted no time getting ready, and soon the message came and they were on their way.

They pulled up in the parking lot outside the port with ten minutes to spare. The closest port to the city was around 2 hours away; in the meantime, 'We made it!'

'But we have to change at Notingo,' Malkmus reminded him. As soon as the ship was on its way, a hot breakfast was served. To the staff, Malkmus, hiding, reached the place and stole some food for all, as all of them had not eaten since last night.

 After eating, the men napped for a couple of hours. When they awoke, they took out the map Onlow had drawn. 'It shows the area around.' they remarked, studying it closely. 'But I don't know how to get there.'

They reached the port and tried the port counter. A clerk there started asking them about how they had travelled on a cargo ship without a ticket or permission.

 Just then, a quiet voice behind them asked, 'Are you Vanlo?' He turned to face the speaker, a well-dressed man in a dark suit.

'Yes.' he replied.

'My name is Ray Typhon,' the stranger said. 'I've had a word to discuss with you. I'm going to give you some important reports. Unfortunately, I didn't have time, so would you all stop by my office to get them, so I'll have to ask you to come there with me?'

Typhon, then looking at the port clerk, said they had been called by me and were my guests. Vanlo looked at Malkmus.

They had never heard of anyone by the name of Typhon. The man smiled. 'I'm glad to see you're cautious,' he said. 'But I assure you of no harm.' They realised they did not know anyone here, and to get out of the port, they would have to take this risk.

Mr. Typhon smiled promptly. Then he added seriously, 'The reports are very important; Vanlo and Malkmus knew they would have to risk accompanying him.'

'All right,' Vanlo and Malkmus said. 'Let's go.'

'My car and chauffeur are right outside,' Mr. Typhon told them, walking towards the exit.

All of them followed him to a large black sedan parked outside. The chauffeur leaned back and opened the rear door. They climbed in. Mr. Typhon seated himself in front. The rest of the team was asked to come in a different van waiting at a distance.

Suddenly, as the driver started the motor, both rear doors opened, and two big, tough-looking men slid in, one on each side of Vanlo and Malkmus. Instantly, Vanlo and Malkmus realised this was a trap.

Malkmus reached across to the dashboard in a desperate effort to switch off the engine. The two thugs pushed him back roughly. 'None of that!' one snarled as the car shot away from the port.

'From here on, you will take orders from us. Don't argue, or we'll shut you up in a way you won't like!'

The car moved smoothly through traffic, and the three captors never loosened their grasp. After a long ride, the car reached a wide, store fronted avenue in one of the city's suburbs.

Slowing up, it turned down the street and pulled into the lane of a very "old house near the corner".

The driver parked in the back, and the four men hustled the men inside. 'They went to an open hall protected by a railing. Get in there!' Scarface ordered and pushed the two into a room near the head of the wall.

There was one window with the shade drawn and a table. 'What's this all about?' Vanlo demanded Typhon ignored the question. 'Empty their pockets!' he barked. Scarface opened their hand and pulled the blackjack. Realising that resistance was pointless, they obeyed.

'You won't need this stuff,' Typhon said, as gold, drugs, and keys were laid on the table. Going through Vanlo,

Typhon found the map that Onlow had drawn. Typhon gave them a hard look. Where did you get this?'

'What do you want with us?' Vanlo shouted.

Typhon's eyes glittered menacingly. 'So you won't talk about the map. Well, you will later.' He folded the map and put it on the table.

'They better be interested to hear about this,' he said to his group of men. 'Now tie up these smart alecks.' Suddenly, Malkmus kicked Vanlo. And picked up the map, and both of them jumped out of the window.

They looked down at the earth and whispered, 'Help us, mother. Help us.' They expose themselves. As they would probably be shot instantly, their eyes were looking everywhere. They had to rely on their ears. There were great shooters who could shoot by relying on sound.

They heard a loud yet surprisingly gentle voice. 'Come out; we don't want to hurt you. It's better if-' The voice stopped mid-sentence. It would never be heard again. They kept silent and walked ahead.

They listened intently. Hearing no sound, they threw themselves to the ground, rolling rapidly behind low shrubs. Still no sign of anyone. 'Move! Move! There's nobody else!'

They quickly rose to their feet, sprinted to the group, and ran hard. Towards the temporary opening. They had to kill the other soldier before. They reached them. The temporary opening showed signs of a massive struggle.

Most of the soldiers, except for them, will be caught soon. A giant of a man loomed in front, questioning them. Three soldiers surrounded each one, while two more tried to look for them. 'Answer me!' barked Typhon 'Where are they?'

Typhon continued. 'We can forgive and let both of you go.

Tell us what we want to know. And come out. This is my promise.' While this was going on, one of the members of Vanlo was brought in for interrogation. Typhon signalled one of his members. 'As you command, Typhon.' said the soldier.

Wiping his gun and slipping it back in, he walked up to a member of Vanlo and drew out his knife. He positioned himself behind the man, pulled his head back, and placed the knife against his throat.

Then he looked at Typhon, awaiting the order. Typhon took a look around and shouted again, 'Where are they?' 'You may not care for your own life, Vanlo,' said Typhon, 'But don't you want to save at least your members'?" The member looked at Typhon and shouted, 'I am ready to die, and Vanlo Don't come out or don't say anything!'

Typhon, come out. Come out; I'm saying I'm giving you one last chance. Try to understand. I give you my word. I will not harm you. And I will let you and your men go. Come out and surrender. And give me the map. Vanlo looked here and there; he looked around at a distance. He saw three of his men.

We're being surrounded? And they had guns on their throats. When he looked around again at the gate. He saw his friend. Whose throat was being slit a little bit and blood was coming out.

Then he tried to hide himself behind a car. Suddenly, Malkmus, who was hiding on the other side, told him that we had a chance to escape. They both wanted to try, but Vanlo then realised that if they both escaped, they all would be dead. So he shouted, "I want surrender; free my men.

Typhon said, "Yeah, we shouted in anger; we wish to make you understand. The circumstances that you are in account of the place mentioned we just need to know where the map is. And I promise we shall leave.

I give you my word that you and your men will be free. We just want you to do as we say: hand over the map, and you shall be free. This is a man's word. Vanlo looked around; he could see five soldiers and three cars. He looked at Typhon and said, "You and your men will be free.

 We just want you to do as we say: hand over the map, and you shall be free. This is a man's word. Vanlo looked around; he could see five soldiers and three cars. He looked at Typhon. Together, he and his friend planned. Yeah,

Typhon!" shouted Vanlo in anger. We can do it Vanlo said Malkmus, with what the hell said Vanlo? Somehow, I don't believe him or his words. Got any ideas for humour, Malkmus? Um okay. Okay, I was the choice when you said Vanlo. If we're going to go, I wish we had taken that all with us.

There is nowhere else that you will find a place to go; my gun's Typhon is going to dive deep into the throats of your men and explore it like it has never seen it before. But before we begin the act of this journey, I wish to give you one more final chance to surrender.

 Vanlo stared at the Typhon and his men with unblinking eyes. Typhon continued, 'So I have an offer. Step forward. Tell your friend to also step forward. And we will let this man of yours live. We will even let everyone of you leave unharmed.

All we want is your surrender. 'Vanlo," said Malkmus, remaining unmoved. Silent. The Typhon grazed the gun slowly along one of the men of Vanlo, leaving behind his scarf as a line.

He spoke in a husky manner: 'I don't have all day... Suddenly, Malkmus struck backward, hitting one of the Typhon men. As fast as the wind, Malkmus shut the man's mouth with one hand and, with his other hand on his head, twisted his neck, and the man fell down dead.

Malkmus screamed, 'Run! Run away, Vanlo! I am not worth your life!' Three Typhon men moved in and pushed Malkmus to the ground.

Typhon, after a few moments, moved towards the other member of Vanlo's team and kicked him hard. He surveyed, turning in every direction.

All the time, he kept kicking members of the Vanlo team again and again.

He bent and roughly pulled the poor man to his feet. Vanlo could see the captive now. Clearly. This time Typhon held the head firmly with his right hand, and he held the gun with his other hand.

He placed it on his head. 'I can shoot the Typhon now, and your precious man will be dead in just a few moments. Give up, Vanlo.' He moved the gun to the man's forehead. Or he can bleed to death slowly. All of you have some time to think about it.'

Vanlo was still. He was left alone. It would be foolhardy to try anything. But he could not let Malkmus die. He had been like a brother to him. 'All we want is the map,' yelled Typhon. 'You surrender, and I shall let the rest of them leave. You have my word. You have the word of a boss! 'Let him go!' screamed Vanlo, still hidden behind one of the cars.

'Step forward and surrender,' said Typhon, holding the gun now on Malkmus' forehead. 'And we will let him go.' Vanlo looked down and closed his eyes. With helpless rage. And then, without giving himself any time for second thoughts, he stepped out.

But not before his instincts made him knock out one man of Typhoon, and he picked up his gun, ready to fire. 'Great Typhon, letting go of Malkmus for a moment, and running his hand along at the back of his head it's so kind of you to join us. Where is the map and the other stuff?' Vanlo didn't answer.

Some Typhon men began moving slowly towards Vanlo. He noticed that. They were carrying guns and long sticks, which were good enough to injure but not kill. He stepped forward and lowered the gun he had.

'I am surrendering. Let Malkmus and others go.' Typhon laughed softly as he pushed the figure deep into the trigger and shot Malkmus. Gently, slowly. The Typhon went through the head from left to right, never stopping. 'No!' screamed Vanlo.

He raised his gun and shot deep into Typhon. It punctured the jacket and lodged itself instantly in a tree. 'I want him alive!' screamed Typhon from behind the protective Malkmus body. More of Typhon's men joined those already moving towards Vanlo.

TYPHON!' shouted Vanlo as he pulled another gunshot from his gun, quickly nocked it, and shot it, bringing another TYPHON man down instantly. It did not slow the pace of the others. They kept rushing forward.

Vanlo fired another gunshot. His last. One more man to the ground, the others pressed on. 'TYPHON!' Men were almost upon him, their guns raised. 'TYPHON!' screamed Vanlo. As his men closed in, he lassoed his gun.

Vanlo hit back with the gun, straight at one of the men's heads, knocking him off his feet. Alert. One hand held the empty gun in the middle. He was surrounded by at least five or six. But they kept their distance. "Typhon!' bellowed Vanlo, praying.

'We don't want to hurt you, Vanlo,' said a Typhon, surprisingly polite. 'Please surrender. You will not be harmed. Vanlo cast a quick glance at Malkmus. 'Is he still breathing?'

'We have the equipment in our car to save him,' said the TYPHON. 'Don't force us to hurt you.'

'Please.' Vanlo filled his lungs with air and screamed yet again, 'TYPHON!' He thought he heard a faint voice from a long distance. 'Vanlo aa...' A few men moved suddenly from his left, aiming for his legs.

Vanlo jumped high, and while in the air, he quickly released the right-hand grip and hit one of them on the side of his head. Knocking him unconscious. He shouted again, 'TYPHON!" and suddenly one of the TYPHON men hid the back of the gun from behind. Into his back head.

'Ra..." Vanlo fell to his knees and collapsed to the ground. Before he could recover, the other men ran in and held him tight. He struggled fiercely as two of them came forward, holding a rope in their hands.

A blue-coloured paste was held against his nose. As darkness began to envelop him, he sensed some ropes against his hands and feet. And the darkness took over.

chapter 3

Back to First Love

A few years earlier, in East of Hills, Vanlo had travelled a long way through the forest, nearly a hundred miles west of the river. He sought to meet the lady, the virgin beauty. Unfortunately, the darkness had changed the course. It also changed Vanlo's fortunes. To add to Vanlo's vows, the rain failed repeatedly for a few days after the change of course.

The girl looked like an adolescent, perhaps older. She had an unkempt look about her. The stench from her clothes suggested that she had not changed them for a while. She was tall, lean, and surprisingly muscular. Her blue-green shaded eyes and scarred body gave her an eye locking look. She looked at Vanlo. There was a sudden flash of recognition in Vanlo's eyes, as though sensing an opportunity. It is unclear what Vanlo's next move will be, but the introduction of this mysterious girl has piqued his interest. The change of course and the subsequent change in fortune may have opened up new possibilities for him.

Only time will tell what lies ahead for Vanlo and this enigmatic girl.

Vanlo, almost breaking into a desperate run. Praying that this was the correct path he was looking for. He kept running. Until he was forced to stop. Breathless and sweating, he looked around and realized he had reached a dead end. Disappointed and frustrated, he turned around to head back the way he came.

As he walked, he couldn't shake the feeling that he had missed something important. Perhaps he needed to retrace his steps and search more carefully. Whatever it was, Vanlo knew he couldn't give up until he found it. The enigmatic girl's presence had ignited a fire within him, and he was determined to uncover

He halted, confronted by a huge, solid rock wall. He was now truly lost, finding himself at the end of nothing. He was as far as it could be. It was quiet, with scarcely anyone around. The sun had almost set, and there was faint darkness.

He did not know what to do. 'What is there now?' A voice was heard from behind. Vanlo turned around, ready to strike.

He saw five to six wolves moving towards him. He turned and ran, but did not get far. He got stuck out and tripped, making him fall flat on his face. There were more of them. He got up quickly and grabbed his knife. Five had gathered around him.

He remembered the warning about the village people. Of people getting killed up in the forest. But he had not believed those stories, thinking that the wolf never hurt anyone.

Thinking he should have listened to the village people. Looked around nervously. The five wolves were now in front of him. The rock wall was behind him, leaving him with no escape route. He could feel his heart racing as he held on to his knife tightly.

The wolves were circling him, their eyes fixed on him, ready to attack. He knew he had to act fast if he wanted to survive this encounter. He took a step forward, hoping to scare them away, but they didn't budge.

He knew he had to fight for his life. With a deep breath, he lunged forward, ready to defend himself.

There was no escape. He looked at them threateningly. The one in the centre bit a fingernail in mock fear, and Vanlo balanced his knife against his body and quickly pulled back. He pointed the knife at them.

'I know how to use this.' Wolf looked at him, his eyebrows raised. He turned to see that the rock wall was behind him. There was no escape. He moved the knife at them, threatening them.

He moved his knife hand. Ferociously on one of the wolves, clutching his arm. 'I'll break the other one too if you don't get out of here,' growled Vanlo. And the wolf ran. The other four delinquents, however, stood their ground. Gripping his knife, holding it high above, and judging the distance perfectly, he swung his weapon viciously on one wolf's head.

The wolf yelped and fell to the ground, its body writhing in pain. Vanlo felt a surge of adrenaline as he turned to face the remaining three wolves. They were circling him, baring their teeth, and growling menacingly. Vanlo knew that he had to act fast if he wanted to survive this encounter. He took a deep breath and lunged forward, his knife flashing in the sunlight.

The wolves darted to the side, avoiding his attack. Vanlo felt a sharp pain in his side as one of the wolves sank its teeth into his flesh.

The wolf collapsed in a heap, blood spurting from the crack on the back of his head. The three others turned around and rushed forward, trying to grab a bite by the hand. He spread his legs apart and bent, maintaining his balance. Waiting.

For what was to follow. Breathing steady. Suddenly burst forward, going up on legs, spreading it. Ready with the massive teeth in for a grip. Its jaws opened wide, and it headed straight for the hand. Rely on jaws to finish the job. But, to its misfortune, Vanlo was almost ready. With one foot back, his powerful muscles remained on his feet. Using his left hand, he held the wolf by its throat and kept its jaws away.

He could not stop the wolf from clawing his leg. It causes much damage. He pulled his right hand back and thrust the knife deep into the wolf's abdomen.

Its sharp-edged blade sliced in smoothly. The beast is in pain. He pushed the wolf back. The wolf struggled for a few seconds, and then it was dead. Using his left leg, he held the other wolf by its head and gave himself momentum high in the air.

His legs were up, and his knees were close to his chest. Above the ground, his outstretched arms caught a branch. He swung and balanced his way to the rock top smoothly, then slid to the ground on the other side. He took a deep breath and looked around, making sure there were no other wolves nearby.

The forest was quiet, except for the sound of his own heartbeat and breathing. He wiped the sweat from his forehead and felt the adrenaline slowly dissipating. It was not the first time he had faced a pack of wolves, but it was always a dangerous and exhilarating experience.

He checked his backpack and made sure he had everything he needed for the rest of his journey. The sun was already setting, and he had to find a safe place to camp for the night. He started walking,

He began running, his breath heavy. Checking the necessary sound. Of any kind following him. He ran in the direction of the mountain. Without any hesitation. Building up speed as he neared, everything was as it should be. Nothing was amiss.

The journey is now a long and convoluted one. He would need to travel by dusty road. In front of him, in the distance, where the hills began, different streams came in from different directions. He kept on it and slowly reached the mountain; these were the famous red rocked mountains, which were famous for their mischievous magic and illusions.

This was the place where, once reached, no one would ever return. Vanlo had forgotten this, and as he had travelled a long and difficult path, it just did not strike his mind, and he started claiming the red mountains were a difficult and steep climb, but as the man was a person from the farm land and with a good body, he could climb the dangers and steep climb.

On the way, he found an opening, and as he was tired and thirsty, he entered the opening and saw a natural water stream.

As he was very tired, he just reached the water stream and drank a little water, and then, to clean himself, he took a dip in the water. When he came out a few minutes later, he only then realised where he was and what he had done. But it was late; the illusions had already played their part, and in a moment before Vanlo could think of anything, an illusion hit him.

There were strange things happening, and he could hear strange voices. Vanlo had unknowingly entered the dangerous red-rock mountains, known for their mischievous magic and illusions.

'You just take everything. I don't need anything anymore. What about you? I feel so sad. How could he? Well, I found another girl.'

'I dreamed about our marriage every single night. Wait. We're going to be boyfriend and girlfriend. How do you know that? Do you want to take her away from me? What? Why would you want that? This is your decision.'

'I brought you here for today. At that time, I had no idea what secret connected my fiancée and Steve or how they would fight for my heart.'

'My name is Eva, and this is my love story. Will you save me?'

'Hope so. Sorry, the finest champagne for my girlfriend, please. Please, shh.'

'Let him say that he's not the only one enjoying life, okay? Thanks. To you. In a flash, my fiancée was rushing to her table. However, it turned out that it was not for me. Well, well, well. Tommy Johnson.'

'What the hell are you doing here? Zach, after those years, I wouldn't think you recognised me. As you are out of prison, I hope you had a great time there. You know each other? If you don't believe me, what the hell are you doing with this criminal? It's none. Of your business. Actually, it is. She's my fiancée. Not anymore. She's. Going.'

'To marry me. What? You cannot marry this guy. He's a criminal. And you're a cheater. Well, she prefers to put up with my cheating brother than me with a scumbag who just came out of prison. Come on, we're leaving.'

'No, I don't want to go with you. What? Yes, I'll marry you.'

'Are you out of your mind? You know what? I don't even care. Have fun, you two. What am I going to do? We're going to celebrate. You're happy now. It's because you finally got back in the car for us; it's true, right?'

'You know nothing. Well. I know that you both used me. Don't forget your bag. I. I didn't realise until I was in the middle of the street that no one needed me and I had nowhere to go. Lost? What do you need? This. Is your bag and a wallet. Second time in one day. Just go to hell. I just can't.'

'Bobby Ray. You're in the wrong neighbourhood. I like your father. Well, yours? Imagine. What the hell is she doing around here alone? With no money? Seriously? What a. Waste of time. Do you.' 'Have a place to spend the night? I was going to answer that question from a man who knows every place in the area.'

'You don't have to. Let's go. Where? You can stay at my place. Are you out of your mind? You stole my bag. You made me break up with my fiancé. I'm not going anywhere with you.'

'So we won't go anywhere. Why? Why do you have to go somewhere? You have a home. You have a bag that everybody wants to steal.'

'God, I couldn't feel my legs anymore. And he was just standing there like everything was fine. Why? Come on. I'm going to get you a form and make you tea that I stole from an Indian.'

'You're an idiot. Maybe, but I seem to be the only one who cares about you now. When I get the form, I'll be straight back. Okay. I hope you do that.'

'In the blink of an eye, he carefully wrapped me in a blanket, gave me warm socks, and treated me to the most delicious wine in the world. I don't remember what we were talking about, but it was so warm and relaxing. I don't even remember falling asleep. But suddenly I remembered where I was and who I was with.'

'Good Morning, Sleeping Beauty. Oh, my God. What? A snake? Do you have Snake here? Why did you jump? Up like that? Did we? Wait, no. You slept. All night. Nothing happened. Don't worry. I should probably go. Wait, chill out. Where do you want to go? I'm going to make you the best breakfast of your life.'

'You can cook? You think all I can do is steal? I suddenly. I noticed that Tom didn't look like a criminal at all. His eyes and smile revealed a good soul.'

'His whole tint at all, except for the layer of a dangerous thief, Good choice. So strange. What? No, you feel good. It's just that your life looks like a normal person's life. You know, like family, friends, and books but somehow you became a thief. You know, stuff happens. That's enough. About that.'

'You say that as if you had to become a criminal. I really you think so? What do you know about that? I would really like to have a normal education, a good job, and a chance to take a pretty girl to a fancy restaurant. A girl who wouldn't think of me as a thief.'

'Listen, I... I just meant that we're both adults, and we get to choose what we want to do with our lives. So you also chose your fiancée to cheat on you? Wait, no. I got. There's nothing else to say. I just.'

Think that even if bad stuff happened to you in the past, it doesn't have to predict your future. You can still, if you want, invite a beautiful, intelligent girl to dinner. Just do it. I had.'

'Only known Tom for a day. But for some reason, I was so nervous that I couldn't sit still. Mostly, I couldn't wait for him to come home. Tom, I'm sorry. How did you find me?'

'Oh, my God. Did you forget? Get your things, and let's go. I'm not going anywhere. With you. Monty is a criminal. He's just using you to get revenge on me. That's not true. It is true. I'm the reason he ended.'

Vanlo's head started to spin like a giant wheel, and he fell to the ground. He would have woken after a few hours; the effect of the voice had not yet gone, and to his surprise, he saw a huge reptile in front of him, looking at him in surprise, he saw a huge reptile in front of him, looking at him intently.

It was unlike anything he had ever seen before, with scales that shimmered in the sunlight and eyes that glinted with intelligence. Vanlo couldn't help but feel a sense of awe and wonder as he gazed at the creature before him. As he slowly regained his senses, he realised that this was no ordinary reptile—it was a dragon.

And with that realisation, Vanlo's life was forever changed. From that moment on, he knew that he had a destiny to fulfil.

Vanlo's heart raced as he tried to make sense of what was happening. He wondered if he was hallucinating or if this was some sort of bizarre dream.

But as he looked closer, he realised that the reptile was real and that it seemed to be communicating with him.

Vanlo felt a mixture of fear and curiosity as he tried to figure out what the creature wanted. He cautiously approached the reptile and was surprised when it spoke to him in a language he had never heard.

The minute Vanlo had his eyes locked on it, the reptile took hold of Vanlo and made a huge jump, taking them both to a different dimension. Vanlo was in shock, but he knew that this was his destiny unfolding before him.

 He had been chosen for a great purpose, and he was ready to embrace it. From that moment on, Vanlo's life would never be the same. He had a new world to explore, new challenges to face, and a new destiny to fulfil.

And into the water it went, disappearing from sight. Vanlo stood there for a moment, processing what had just happened, before turning to face the new world that lay before him.

He took a deep breath and stepped forward, ready to embrace his destiny and all the adventures that awaited him.

 With a newfound sense of purpose, Vanlo stepped forward into the unknown, ready to face whatever challenges lay ahead. He knew that he had been chosen for a great purpose, and he was determined to fulfil it.

As he explored this new world, he encountered strange creatures and obstacles that tested his courage and determination. But with each challenge, he grew stronger and more confident in his abilities. And as he continued on his journey, he knew that he was destined for greatness. For Vanlo,

Vanlo could not understand what was going on, where he had been taken, or how even in water he was able to breathe and be comfortable.

But as he stood there, he realised that he had a choice to make. He could either dwell on his confusion and fear or embrace this new world and all the possibilities it held. With a deep breath,

Vanlo chose the latter. He stepped forward with determination, ready to face whatever challenges lay ahead and discover the secrets of this mysterious place. And as he journeyed deeper into this world, he knew that he was on the path to fulfilling his destiny. But despite his confusion, Vanlo knew that he had to keep moving forward and face whatever challenges came his way.

He trusted that there was a reason he had been brought to this new world and that he had a purpose to fulfil. With a sense of determination and a willingness to learn, Vanlo embraced his new surroundings and began his journey towards greatness. The reptile reached a place, stopped, and passed through Vanlo in a white ball nearby. Vanlo watched in amazement as the reptile disappeared into the distance, leaving him with a sense of wonder and excitement.

He knew that he was on the right path and that there was much to discover in this new world. With renewed vigour, he continued his journey, eager to uncover the secrets that lay ahead and fulfil his destiny. As he walked, he couldn't help but feel grateful for the opportunity to explore this mysterious place and for the strength and courage that had brought him this far.

Once upon a time, there lived a king and queen who loved each other dearly. In this world, but the queen cheated the king and had an affair with a commoner. The king was heartbroken and banished the queen from the kingdom. She left, taking their child with her.

The child grew up in a faraway land, unaware of their true identity. But fate had a way of bringing them back to their rightful place. One day, the child stumbled upon a clue that led them back to their kingdom. With determination and a sense of purpose, they set out on a journey to reclaim their throne and restore peace, and they had an affair with a nobleman.

The king eventually found out and was devastated. He banished the queen and her lover from the kingdom and ruled alone for many years. However, he never forgot the pain and betrayal he had experienced, and it weighed heavily on his heart.

Despite his success as a ruler, he was never truly happy again. The lesson to be learned from this story is that trust is a precious commodity, and once it is broken, it can be difficult to repair.

One day the King was sitting alone by the side of a waterfall that sprung from some rocks in the large park adjoining the castle. He was feeling more miserable than usual and had sent away his guards so that no one might witness her grief.

Suddenly he heard a rustling movement in the lake below the waterfall, and, on glancing up, he saw a large tortoise climbing on to a stone beside him.

'Great King,' said the tortoise, 'I am here to tell you that the desire of your heart will soon be granted. But first, you must permit me to lead you to the palace of the dark, which, though hard to find, has never been seen by mortal eyes because of the thick clouds that surround it.'

'When there, you will know more; that is, if you will trust yourself to me.'

The king had never before heard a tortoise speak and was struck dumb with surprise. However, he was so enchanted at the words of the tortoise that he smiled sweetly and held

out his hand; it was taken, not by the tortoise,
Which had stood there only a moment before, but by a little woman smartly dressed in black and crimson with a blue ribbon. The woman ran down a path along which the king had been a hundred times before, but it seemed so different that he could hardly believe it was the same. Instead of having to push her way through nettles. The trees were so tall and thick that, even at midday,
'What can it be?' He asked, turning to him:
'Oh, that is the dark palace, and here are some of them coming to meet us.'
As he spoke, the gates swung back, and six dark signs approached, each bearing in their hand a white ball and saying nothing. The king was both fascinated and frightened by their appearance, but he trusted their words and followed their lead.

As they entered the dark palace, the king realized that he had entered a world unlike anything he had ever seen before.

The white balls carried by the dark signs turned out to be magical orbs that illuminated the palace with a soft, eerie light. The king felt a sense of wonder and awe as he explored the palace and met its mysterious inhabitants.

They told the king he needed to feed the ball with people if the person was worthy. That person will fulfil his destiny. The king was hesitant at first. He began to search for someone who would be willing to sacrifice themselves for his cause. Eventually, he found a brave and loyal subject who was willing to offer their life for the good of the kingdom. The king fed the magical orb, but nothing happened.

So they waited for the right time, and this is how Vanlo got into the magical orb. As he was a very good soul, the orb started to glow brighter and brighter, and the dark side emerged, revealing its true form. The king and his subjects were horrified as the orb transformed into a powerful, malevolent entity that threatened to destroy the kingdom.

The king now knew that the kingdom would not last anymore, so he changed his size to a smaller reptile, got himself stuck to the neck of Vanlo, and transferred himself into his body in order to fight against the evil entity from within.

The battle was long and intense, but in the end, the king emerged victorious, and the kingdom was saved. Vanlo was hailed as a hero, and the king returned to his original form, grateful for the sacrifice that had been made.

From that day on, the kingdom prospered under the wise and just rule of the king and the bravery of Vanlo.

The king still could not forget the backbiting of his wife, the queen, so he decided one day that to take revenge, he would kill all the women who were not truthful, and so he called upon his trusted men and told them that from tomorrow on, all nine members of the kingdom would be ruling.

The king would go on his personal achievements on the basis of Vanlo. After signing the ritual, he changed his shape into a naga and placed himself on the right hand of Vanlo. As a tattoo, and then the unbelievable happened. Like a missile from a submarine, Vanlo was shot out of the sea onto the earth's surface.

Three days later, Vanlo lay unconsumed on the beach under a coconut tree, and on the fourth day, a coconut fell and was cut in half midway through, spilling all its water on the face of Vanlo. Despite the king's previous victory and the prosperity of the kingdom, his desire for revenge led to a cruel and unjust decision.

 He planned to kill all women who were not truthful, and he handed over the rule of the kingdom to nine members, including himself, in the form of a Naga tattoo on Vanlo's hand. However, Vanlo was suddenly shot out of the sea and washed up on a beach, where he remained unconscious for several days until a coconut fell and revived him. The fate of the curse

Vanlo got up and went and sat under a tree on the rock, contemplating the events that had just transpired. He realized that his desire for revenge had grown in him and that his hatred for women had been on top of his mind. However, the coconut falling on his face was a sign from the heavens that he needed to change his ways and abandon his cruel intentions. Vanlo decided to renounce his Naga tattoo, and his transformation took place in front of his eyes. The tattoo leapt from his neck and emerged as King Kaiman.

King Kaiman started speaking to Vanlo. Vanlo was in a fix; he could not understand what the king was saying. He did not understand a single word, as the language he was speaking in was not the one Vanlo understood in the end,

Vanlo realized that the curse that had plagued him for years had been lifted. He felt a sense of relief and gratitude towards the heavens for showing him the error of his ways. He knew that he had to embrace this new chapter of his life with open arms and learn to be a better person. With King Kaiman by his side, Vanlo felt a sense of purpose and direction.

He knew that he had a lot to learn, but he was ready to face the But Vanlo's hope was short lived, as what he thought was total wrong was that the king then hit Vanlo's forehead with his tongue. Vanlo was left bewildered and confused once again. He couldn't make sense of what had just happened. He wondered if he had offended the king in some way or if he had misunderstood the situation entirely.

Despite his confusion, Vanlo knew that he couldn't let this setback deter him from his journey towards self-improvement.

He would have to find a way to communicate with the king and learn from him, no matter how difficult it may be. Vanlo took a deep breath and prepared the king once again hit Vanlo hard with his tongue on the forehead, and he fell down in pain.

Vanlo realized that the king was not going to be an easy teacher, but he was determined to learn from him nonetheless. He got up, dusted himself off, and approached the king once again, ready to try and communicate in a different way. Despite the challenges he faced,

Vanlo remained committed to his journey towards self-improvement and was determined to learn all he could from the king, no matter how difficult it might be. This time, the king hit it harder with his tail, a sting from Vanlo's lower neck, and a liquid in the spinal vein. Despite the pain, Vanlo refused to give up.

He knew that the road to self-improvement was never easy, but he was willing to endure any challenge to achieve his goals. With a newfound determination, Vanlo stood up once again and faced the king, ready to learn and grow from his teachings. He knew that the journey ahead would be difficult, but he was ready to face it head-on.

After standing his ground in front of the king for ten to fifteen minutes, he fell unconscious on the ground. Despite the setback, Vanlo's determination remained unwavering.

He knew that the path to self-improvement was not a linear one, and setbacks were inevitable. However, he refused to let this discourage him and was determined to continue his journey towards growth and enlightenment.

With a renewed sense of purpose, Vanlo picked himself up and continued on his path, ready to face whatever challenges lay ahead. After some time, when he came back to consciousness, he looked around, but the king was not to be found. Undeterred, Vanlo continued on his path, determined to apply the lessons he had learned from the king and become the best version of himself.

He knew that the journey would not be easy, but he was ready to face any obstacle that came his way. As he walked forward, he felt a sense of peace and purpose, knowing that he was on the right path. And although he never saw the king again, he knew that the lessons he had learned from him would stay with him.

He reached a lake of fresh water because he was tired and had not eaten for a long time.

He went ahead and drank some water from the lake and tried to clean himself, and what hit his eye was a shock.

The reptile king entered and became a part of his right hand, and now his right hand had the live reptile wrapped around it.

Vanlo was surprised and confused, not knowing what to do. But then he remembered the lessons he had learned

from the king: to face his fears and embrace the unknown. He decided to accept the reptile as a part of him and use it to his advantage. With the reptile's agility and strength,
Vanlo was able to accomplish feats he never thought possible. He became known as the Reptile Warrior, and his legend spread far and wide. And although he never
He travelled and reached the red mountains now to search for his lady love. He knew that the reptile king would always be with him, guiding him on his journey.
Vanlo had embraced the unknown and found strength in it, and he was ready for whatever challenges lay ahead.
He climbed the red mountains, and when he reached the top of the mountain, he saw a tree with all blue leaves, pink flowers, and black fruits growing on it. He knew that this was a sign. With the Reptile Warrior by his side,
Vanlo had learned that sometimes the things that scare us the most can also be the things that give us the most strength and power. And with this knowledge, he was able to
conquer any obstacle that came before Vanlo could think of any future, he saw the reptile king slowly start moving and trying to make his way out of Vanlo's body, which had not happened for a few months in his journey.
Vanlo realized the reptile king's power over the red mountains. He knew that he had to release the reptile king from his body so that he could fulfil his destiny as ruler of the red mountains.
His heart started pumping heavily. Vanlo could feel the reptile king trying to push himself out of his body, and there was a thudding sound. Winds started blowing, and huge thunderstorms hit the red mountains. Vanlo could not wait any longer, as the pain his body was feeling was

really stressful, as if he were leaving and dying a thousand times.

really stressful, as if he were leaving and dying a thousand times.

chapter 4

Back to First

He closed his eyes, as the pain was now unbearable. All his energy was draining, and suddenly a powerful lightning storm hit Vanlo's arm, releasing the reptile king from his body. With a final burst of power, the reptile king emerged from Vanlo's body and stood before him, majestic and powerful.

The reptile king gave a loud shout that gave him a sense of relief. A lightning storm again hit the reptile king as Vanlo watched him disappear into the mountains. With his newfound strength and power, the reptile king had finally been freed from Vanlo's body, and Vanlo was left feeling exhausted but relieved.

 He knew that he had accomplished something great and that he could now move forward with renewed strength and determination. As he looked out at the red mountains, he felt a sense of peace and gratitude for the experience he had just gone through.

The winds had calmed down, and the thunderstorms had passed. Vanlo took a deep breath and began to make his way down the mountain,

With the guidance and strength he had provided, Vanlo knew that he had grown and changed in ways he never thought possible. As the reptile king slowly started giving a huge cry,

He knew that he had completed his mission. He felt a sense of fulfilment and satisfaction, as he knew that he had grown both mentally and emotionally and was ready to face any challenges that lay ahead.

With a renewed sense of purpose, Vanlo looked forward to the next chapter of his journey. The reptile king slowly started moving down from Vanlo's body to the ground and then jumped over the wall of the window, disappearing into the night.

Vanlo watched in awe as the creature disappeared, wondering where it was headed and what other mysteries this world held.

He couldn't wait to explore and discover more about this strange move. However, at that time, there was a celestial voice that spoke, 'Abandon this place. He will be very superior in strength and power and a very fortunate person. You can't kill him now.'

Vanlo's was taken aback by the sudden voice and wondered who it belonged to. He couldn't shake off the feeling that there was more to this encounter than he initially thought. With a sense of curiosity and caution, he made a mental note to keep an eye out for any signs of the reptile king or any other mysterious beings that may cross his path in the future.

As he walked away from the window, Vanlo's couldn't help but feel a sense of excitement for the adventures that lay ahead.

Typhon and his men were also very nervous as to what was happening, as they could see no one in or outside where they were stationed. They too were left wondering about the mysterious voice and what it meant for their mission. Despite their unease, they followed Vanlo's as he led them away from the building and towards their next destination, ready to face whatever challenges lay ahead.

'The person who will kill him is already born.' The words echoed in Vanlo's' mind as he walked, wondering what they could possibly mean. He couldn't help but feel a sense of foreboding, but also a strange sense of destiny.

He knew that his journey was far from over and that he would have to remain vigilant and prepared for whatever came his way. With a deep breath, he pushed aside his doubts and focused on the path ahead, determined to fulfil his mission and uncover the truth behind the mysterious voice.

He knew that he was not going to be able to misguide Typhon and his men forever and that eventually they would catch up to him. But for now, he had a job to do, and he would do it to the best of his abilities.

As they walked, he couldn't help but wonder who the person was that was destined to slay him. Was it someone he knew? Or a complete stranger? He knew that he couldn't dwell on it for too long, as it would only distract him from his mission.

So he pushed the thought to the back. It was not long before the reptile king and his few men appeared and stood in front of Typhon and his men, ready for the exchange. The tension in the air was palpable as the two groups faced each other, each waiting for the other to make the first move.

The user knew that this was a critical moment, and he had to stay focused if he wanted to come out of it alive. With a deep breath, he stepped forward and began the negotiations, hoping that he could strike a deal that would satisfy both parties.

As the conversation went on, he could feel the weight of Typhon's gaze. The reptile king and his men could not do anything; all they could do was create fear in their minds, but beyond this, they were helpless as they could not fight as they were outnumbered.

The Typhon and his men used this to their advantage and were able to secure a deal that would benefit them.

The exchange was complete, the tension dissipated, and both groups parted ways.

The Typhon's men felt a sense of relief wash over them as they realized they had successfully completed their mission. They knew that they couldn't let their boss down just yet, as there may be more challenges ahead, but for now, they could take a moment to breathe and appreciate his accomplishment.

Vanlo was pushed into a room and beat up badly. They kept asking him about the stuff and where the hell he had kept it, but he refused to speak. Eventually, they gave up and left him there, bruised and battered.

He knew he had to come up with a plan to get out of there and retrieve the stolen goods before it was too late. As he lay there, he couldn't help but think about the Typhon and their power. He knew he had to be careful, but he also knew he couldn't back down.

He had to fight for what was his and make sure justice was served. Vanlo had been beaten up and left in a room by Typhon's assailants, who were after his stolen goods. Despite the danger, he was determined to retrieve what was his and bring the culprits to justice.

He knew he had to be cautious, but he couldn't let fear hold him back. He was ready to fight for his rights and prove that he was not to be messed with. In the meantime, the retile king entered the room through the window. Vanlo and the king started a dialog in the reptile language. Together, they came up with a plan to take down Typhon and his gang and retrieve

Vanlo's stolen goods. What Vanlo understood of the dialog was that the king had no power without the red mountain or any part of the red mountain. With the help of the reptile king, Vanlo felt more confident in his mission to take down Typhon and retrieve his stolen goods.

He knew that the red mountain was a crucial element in their plan, and he was determined to find a way to obtain it. With caution and bravery, Vanlo was ready to face whatever challenges lay ahead and prove that he was not to be underestimated.

Suddenly, Vanlo remembered that while leaving the red mountain, he had picked a sharp eye cauterising stone that was half red and half white. This stone could potentially be a key element in their plan to retrieve the red mountain.

Vanlo shared this information with the reptile king, and together they brainstormed how to use it to their advantage.

With this new information and the support of the reptile king, Vanlo felt more determined than ever to take down Typhon and retrieve what was rightfully his. He knew that the road ahead would not be easy, but he was ready for whatever challenges lay ahead.

Vanlo told the reptile king that when he and his friends were brought here, he had the stone in his pocket, and when they were being brutally tortured one of the Typhon's men had ripped off his coat and thrown it out the window.

He asked the reptile king to check the area outside the window to see if he could find it. The king said it would show itself if both the king and the stone were nearby each other, and he agreed to help Vanlo search for it. The reptile king set out on a mission to find the cauterising stone to take down Typhon and retrieve the red mountain. With determination, ready to face whatever challenges lay ahead. The reptile king went out of the window and started moving in the direction Vanlo had told him about.

Vanlo waited anxiously, hoping that the stone would be found soon. He knew that time was of the essence and that every moment counted. As he waited, he thought about his friends and how they were killed. He knew that to save him, they would risk their lives. Finally,

The reptile king found the cauterising stone. As soon as the king touched the stone, there came a thunder storm and winds started blowing at a higher speed, which became uncontroversial seeing this site outside his window.

Vanlo breathed a sigh of relief. With the power regained by the reptile king and his army, they were able to defeat their enemies and restore the land. Vanlo was grateful for the sacrifice his friends had made and vowed to never forget their bravery.

He knew that their memory would live on and inspire him to continue fighting for what was right. With a newfound sense of support for the reptile king, Vanlo set out on a new adventure, ready to face whatever challenges lay ahead.

The reptile king and his men had not killed Typhon and his few men but had, in fact, captured them and put them in a room with no windows or doors, ensuring they could not escape. The reptile king wanted to show his true colours and give Typhon a chance to redeem himself.

He hoped that Typhon would see who the reptile king really was in his ways and join him in his quest. Only time would tell if Typhon would accept the offer and become an ally or remain an enemy.

But for now, the don and his empire in the city had been defeated, and the reptile king had emerged victorious.

Typhon and his few men had seen the ugly side of the reptile king and knew that the king was not a common person but a beast from hell. Vanlo, on the other hand, saw a different side of the reptile king and had no choice but to follow.

As the reptile king would now do all the wrong things that he did under the ocean, and Vanlo knew his body was now under the control of the reptile king. The future was uncertain, but one thing was for sure: the reptile king had made his mark and would not be forgotten anytime soon.

The future was uncertain, but Vanlo knew that he had no choice as he embarked on a new adventure, he was filled with a sense of purpose and determination. The reptile king and his men would continue to follow him and give him the strength to face whatever challenges lay ahead. The battle had just begun.

Horrifying voices and dangerous visions would not let Typhon and his men sit or sleep. They knew that they had to act fast and stop the reptile king before he caused any more harm. Typhon and his men were ready to face any challenge that came their way, no matter how dangerous it may have been. They were determined to put an end to the reptile king's reign of terror and restore peace for themselves.

But their thoughts and work were short lived as the mentally horrifying things the king did to them made them unable to take it any longer, and eventually, Typhon and his men succumbed to the reptile king's power.

 The battle had ended in defeat, but Typhon's memory would live on as a symbol of bravery and determination in the face of adversity. The reptile king could not live on the land in his original appearance for very long,

So he used the power of stone and sent them back, and he himself changed his size and merged himself with Vanlo's body as a tattoo on his neck again, and he also took the stone with him, so now the tattoo was like a reptile climbing the stone.

The reptile king could now communicate with Vanlo as their minds were connected, and he could control him from within. Typhon and his men surrendered and started to take orders from Vanlo, which was an indirect command from the reptile king.

They may have lost the battle, but their sacrifice was not in vain. Their bravery and determination would inspire others not to stand up against the reptile king and his reign of terror. The fight for the conquest of other cities and other unseen underworld lords was in the making.

A weather-stained canvas stood at the base of some irregularly ascending hills. A footpath wound its way gently down the sloping land till it reached the broad river bottom; creeping through the long swamp grasses that bent over it on either side, it came out on the edge of the Missouri. The scene had shifted to a different setting, away from the battle between Typhon's men and the reptile king.

The description of the weather-stained canvas wigwam and the footpath leading to the river bottom paints a picture of a serene and peaceful environment. However, the mention of the fight for the conquest of other cities and the unseen underworld lords hints at the continuation of the story's conflict and danger.

"Well, it happened on the day we moved camp." The peaceful setting described in the previous sentence is abruptly interrupted as the user introduces the fact that something happened on the day they moved camp. This suggests that the story is about to take another turn, and the reader can expect more action and excitement to come.

The reptile kings ordered Vanlo to return to the place where he was in search of the blue-grey-eyed girl from the woods the mention of the reptile king's order to Vanlo to find the girl from the woods adds to the suspense and intrigue of the story. It implies that there is a larger plot at play and that Vanlo's search for the girl may lead to further conflict and danger. The user's input leaves the reader wanting to know more about the characters and their motivations and eager to see how the story will unfold.

So Vanlo, with a few men, started on the journey to find the girl. This sentence concludes the user's input by providing more information on Vanlo's mission to find the girl. It also sets the stage for the next part of the story, where Vanlo and his men embark on their journey. The reader is left wondering what challenges they will face and if they will be successful in their quest. Overall, the user's input adds depth and complexity to the story, making it more engaging and intriguing for the reader.

Vanlo reached a place where a group of loins were resting, and the sound of a stick breaking on the ground woke them up. The lions immediately stood up and started to approach Vanlo. He knew he had to act fast to avoid being attacked. Vanlo quickly scanned his surroundings for any potential escape routes. He spotted a nearby tree and ran towards it, climbing up as fast as he could. The lions roared and circled the tree, but Vanlo stayed calm and waited for them to lose interest. After a few tense minutes, the lions wandered off, and Vanlo breathed a sigh of relief. He knew he had narrowly escaped a dangerous situation and vowed to be more careful in the future.

When Vanlo was thinking this, his men, who had gone in search of water, were returning when they saw Vanlo climbing down a tree. They rushed towards him, asking what had happened Vanlo quickly recounted his encounter with the lions and how he had managed to escape. His men were relieved to see that he was safe and congratulated him on his quick thinking. They all agreed to be more cautious in the future and to always be on the lookout for potential dangers. With that, they continued on their journey, grateful for their narrow escape.

But they had short lived their happiness as the group of loins, which had gone and returned, got the smell of humans. They began to follow the group, stalking them from a distance. Vanlo and his men remained vigilant, constantly scanning the area for any signs of danger. As they travelled further into the wilderness, the lions grew bolder and began to close in on the group. Vanlo knew that they needed to act fast if they wanted to survive. With his quick thinking and bravery, he led his men on a daring escape, narrowly avoiding the deadly predators.

In the early morning, our simple breakfast was spread on the grass west of our tepee. At the farthest point of the shade, my men sat beside the fire, toasting a piece of dried meat. Near them sat Vanlo, eating his dried meat with unleavened bread and drinking strong black coffee. Despite the close encounter with the lions, Vanlo and his men were able to successfully escape and enjoy a simple breakfast in the wilderness. Their quick thinking and bravery allowed them to survive the dangerous situation and continue on their journey.

Overall, Vanlo and his men faced a dangerous situation with the lions while travelling through the wilderness. However, with Vanlo's quick thinking and bravery, they were able to escape the predators and enjoy a simple breakfast in the morning. Their survival is a testament to their strength and resilience in the face of danger. It is clear that Vanlo is a skilled leader who is able to think on his feet and make quick decisions that ultimately saved his men's lives. This experience will undoubtedly stay with them for the rest of their journey, serving as a reminder of the dangers that lie ahead and the importance of staying alert and prepared at all times. Despite the challenges they may face, Vanlo and his men are determined to continue.

There were eight men going east Among Vanlo were three young braves, two tall girls, and us three little ones, Judéwin, Thowin, and I. We had been very impatient to start on our journey to the Red Mountains, which, we were told, lay a little beyond the great circular horizon of the Western Prairie. Under a sky of rosy apples, we dreamed of roaming as freely and happily as we had chased the cloud shadows on the Dakota plains. We had anticipated much pleasure from a ride on the iron horse, but the throngs of staring palefaces disturbed and troubled us.

 Vanlo's eyes are downcast, daring only now and then to shoot long glances around. Chancing quite breathless upon seeing one familiar object

It was the signal of a familiar landmark that we had passed before on our way to the Red Mountains. Our hearts lifted with hope and excitement, and we knew that we were getting closer to our destination. Despite the discomfort of being surrounded by strangers, we were determined to continue our journey and fulfil

Entering the north, the mountain way close against the wall. The strong, glaring light in the large, whitewashed our eyes. Despite the discomfort and challenges of our journey, we were filled with determination and excitement as we approached our destination. The familiar landmarks gave us hope and lifted our spirits, and we were eager to continue on our path. Even though we were surrounded by unfamiliar faces and felt out of place, we remained steadfast in our pursuit of fulfilment. As we entered the north and the mountains loomed closer, a bright light washed over us, signalling the start of a new adventure.

 Our hearts raced with anticipation as we imagined all the possibilities that lay ahead. The rugged terrain and unpredictable weather did not deter us, for we knew that every obstacle we overcame would bring us closer to our goal. With each step we took, we grew more determined and resilient, ready to face whatever challenges lay ahead.

As we journeyed deeper into the mountains, we felt a sense of awe and wonder at the majestic beauty that surrounded us. We knew that this adventure would be one to remember for a lifetime.

The air grew colder as we ascended higher into the peaks, but our spirits remained high. We could see the snow-capped summits in the distance, beckoning us closer. Our excitement grew with each passing moment, and we knew that we were on the cusp of something truly incredible. The wind howled around us, but we pressed on, determined to reach the summit. We knew that the journey would be difficult, but we also knew that the reward would be worth it. With each step we took, we felt ourselves growing stronger and more resilient, ready to face whatever lay ahead.

Small-voiced men lived in this part of the jungle Startled by the unexpected voice, one of Vanlo's men jerked and fell down, and everyone came to a halt. It was a stark contrast to the excitement and determination we had felt just moments before.

We quickly realized that we were not alone in this wilderness, and the presence of the Small Voice Men added an element of uncertainty to our journey. But we refused to let fear overcome us. We would face whatever challenges came our way, just as we had done before. With renewed focus, we continued on our path, ready to conquer any obstacle that stood in our way.

As we pushed deeper into the jungle, the sounds of the Small Voice Men grew louder and more frequent. We could hear them whispering in the trees and rustling through the underbrush. It was clear that they were watching us, and we couldn't help but feel a sense of unease. But we knew that we couldn't let our guard down. We had come too far to let a few mysterious voices scare us off. We pressed on, our determination growing stronger with each passing moment. And as we approached our destination, we knew that we had overcome yet another challenge in our quest.

The jungle men had already rounded Vanlo and his men from all sides, and there was not even a narrow chance of escape.

But we were not afraid. We had faced danger before, and we were ready to face it again. We drew our weapons and prepared for battle. The Small Voice Men may have had the advantage of surprise, but we had the advantage of strength and skill. We charged forward, ready to defend ourselves and complete our mission. The battle was fierce, but in the end, Vanlo and his men were captured by the Small Voice Men.

Vanlo was relieved to see that none of the team members were seriously injured, although a few had some minor cuts and bruises. They were all tidied up, each one tidied by his hand and leg, and left hanging on a bamboo between two trees, waiting for further instructions from the king of the tribe. Despite the situation, Vanlo and his men remained determined to find a way out and complete their mission. They knew that they couldn't give up now and were prepared to do whatever it took to succeed.

The chief arrived, accompanied by a witch known for her powerful magic. The witch examined Vanlo's men, and with a wave of her hand, one of them was called for in front of her and the chief. The tension was palpable as everyone watched to see what would happen next. The Vanlo man stepped forward, his heart pounding with fear and anticipation. The witch whispered some incantations, and suddenly, the man began to convulse and scream in agony. The chief looked on with a stoic expression, as if this were just another routine punishment. The rest of the team looked on in horror.

The injuries to Vanlo and his men increased more and more every day. It was clear that the witch's magic was not to be trifled with and that the consequences of crossing the chief were severe. The team knew they had to tread carefully if they wanted to survive in this land. They had heard stories of the chief's ruthlessness and the witch's powers, but seeing them first-hand was a whole other level of fear. They wondered how they would ever be able to complete their mission and escape this place alive.

Every day, one of Vanlo's men would be dropped from the hanging tree and sent into the cottage of the witch, never to be seen again. The team knew they couldn't afford to lose any more members. They needed to come up with a plan, and fast. But with the chief's and the witch's power, it seemed like an impossible task. The team huddled together, their minds racing with ideas and fear. They knew they had to act soon before it was too late.

The toucher had been so bad that Vanlo and his men had gone without food and water for many days, weakening them even further. But they couldn't let their physical state hold them back. They had to push through and find a way to defeat the witch and her army.

It was a daunting task, but they were determined to succeed. They took a deep breath and began to strategize, hoping that their plan would be enough to save their lives and complete their mission.

There were days when, if the small voice men and their army could not have a successful day on the hunt, one of the Vanlo men would be taken down and feasted upon by the whole tribe. Despite the constant threat of danger and the harsh conditions they faced, the team remained resolute in its goal. They knew that failure was not an option and that they had to do whatever it took to survive.

 Once, it so happened that one of Vanlo's men reminded Vanlo that he was the choice of the reptile king and that if, for some reason, the reptile king was awakened, he would surely come to their aid. With this reminder, the team found renewed hope and continued on with even greater determination. They knew that they had to keep pushing forward, no matter what obstacles they faced, and that their ultimate success would depend on their ability to work together and stay focused on their goal.

Once, it so happened that there was a big ritual that was to be performed, and a human sacrifice was to be given to appease the gods. Vanlo knew that he had to act fast and come up with a plan to save his man, who was the chosen one and was to be sacrificed. He quickly devised a plan and had to execute it flawlessly, managing to save everyone and escape without being detected.

 Vanlo was working hard to come up with an idea to save his man, and what he got was disappointment. Despite his efforts, Vanlo was unable to come up with a viable plan to save his man. The disappointment was palpable, but the team knew that they could not dwell on it. They had to keep their focus on the task at hand. Failure was not an option, and they had to do whatever it took to survive.

 Now, winter the snow lay deep on the ground in the north. The wind came howling from the Land of Ice. The team knew that they had to brace themselves for the harsh winter ahead. They couldn't afford to waste any more time on disappointment or regret. They had to push forward and continue to work together to overcome the challenges that lay ahead.

Vanlo may not have been able to save his man, but he had to stay strong for the rest of the team. They were all in this together, and they had to keep each other motivated and focused. The snow and wind were just the beginning of their problems ahead.

The hunter tribe from this ice land, who came to know that East Small Voice men had caught some men in the lower forest of the red mountain, also wanted these people to sacrifice to their fire god, so Small Voice men and their king knew they had to be cautious and prepared for any potential threats from the hunter tribe. They couldn't let their guard down, even for a moment. They had to stay alert and ready to face whatever challenges lay ahead, both from the harsh winter weather and from any potential enemies they might encounter. With their determination and teamwork, they were confident that they could overcome any obstacle and reach their goal.

The Small Voice tribe king ordered the witch to do the needful at lightning speed so they could give the hunter tribe a run for their capture over Vanlo and his men.

The witch quickly got to work, using her powers to create powerful protective spells and enchantments to keep the Small Voice tribe safe from harm. With their defences fortified and their spirits high, the tribe set out on their journey, ready to face whatever lay ahead. They knew that it wouldn't be easy, but they were determined to succeed, no matter what.

About fifty small voices, men too, were immobile and silent. It was clear that they were waiting for the witch's protective spells to take effect before they could continue their journey. Despite the harsh winter weather and potential threats from enemies, the Small Voice tribe remained determined and confident in their abilities. With their teamwork and the witch's magical powers, they were ready to face any obstacle and reach their goal. The immobile and silent members of the tribe showed their trust in the witch's abilities and their commitment to the mission at hand.

The North Tribe King ordered his chef priest to please their fire god by offering sacrifices of the best livestock in the tribe. The North tribe King knew that they had to be careful as they were crossing into the territory of the Small Voice tribe, which was known for its ruthless tactics.

However, they remained focused on their goal and were determined to make it to their destination, no matter what obstacles they faced. With their defences fortified and their spirits high, they set out on their journey, ready to overcome any challenge that came their way.

The offering of the North tribe priest was accepted by the fire god, and there was a huge blast, and a huge fire cloud started moving towards the Small Voice tribe. The Small Voice tribe braced themselves for the incoming fire blast, but they were not afraid. They knew that they had the witch's magical powers on their side, and they trusted in their ability to protect themselves. As the fire blast approached, the witch raised her hands and chanted a spell. Suddenly, a wall of water appeared, extinguishing the flames and protecting the tribe from harm. The North tribe King and his followers were shocked at the display of power, but they did not give up.

They knew they had to find a way to defeat the Small Voice tribe and claim the land for their own. They decided to use their own magic to counteract the witch's spells and began to gather their own powerful sorcerers to aid them in their quest.

As they continued on their journey, they encountered many obstacles and challenges, but their determination never wavered. They knew that the fate of their tribe depended on their success, and they were willing to do whatever it took to achieve victory.

The witch called for Vanlo men to be given as sacrifice to their god, but when they were about to make the sacrifice, a voice came in from the distance. It was the voice of a wise elder from a neighbouring tribe who had come to offer his guidance. He explained that sacrificing human lives was not the way to gain favour from the gods and that there were other ways to achieve victory without resorting to violence. The Small Voice tribe and the North Tribal King listened to his words and realized the error of their ways. They agreed to work together and find a peaceful solution to their conflict, and in doing so, they now agreed to split the captured men equally.

Now only Vanlo and his three men were left, and the others were dead. Vanlo and one of his men were given away to the North Tribal, and the other two were kept back with the small voice tribal.

In the end, the Small Voice tribe and the North Tribal King were able to overcome their differences and find a peaceful solution to their conflict. They learned that violence and sacrificing human lives were not ways to gain favour from the gods. Instead, they worked together and split the captured men equally between them. Vanlo and his three men were the only ones left, with Vanlo and one of his men given to the North Tribal and the other two kept with the Small Voice tribe.

But the North Tribal King had different plans in mind; he was a cruel and dangerous man to be believed in. Vanlo and his men were in great danger, and it was uncertain what fate awaited them. The Small Voice tribe, however, had learned the value of peace and cooperation and hoped that their former enemies would eventually see the error of their ways and join them in building a better future for all. Only time would tell what the future held for Vanlo and his men, but for now, the Small Voice tribe could rest easy knowing that they had done their part in promoting peace and unity among their tribe.

chapter 5

Back in the city

Sam banged on the hatch door. Ten men stood at the back. Typhon and Vanlo stood behind everyone with a reassuring look. No one opened the door. Sam Chi looks at Typhon and the Vanlo men standing at the back. Typhon and Vanlo stood behind everyone with a reassuring look. No one opened the door. Sam Chi looks at Typhon and Vanlo. 'Knock again!' ordered Vanlo. 'And harder this time.'

Sam Chi did as ordered. Still, no one opened the door. The tension in the air was palpable as the group waited for a response. The group continued to wait in silence, their nerves on edge as they wondered if anyone would answer the door.

The sound of their own breathing seemed to echo in the stillness. Finally, after what felt like an eternity, a faint shuffling could be heard from inside the house.

Everyone held their breath as the door slowly creaked open, revealing a figure standing in the shadows. The group exchanged a nervous glance, unsure of what was to come next.

A tall, dark, huge man dressed in a three-piece suit came in front and removed his gun, pointing at Sam. Sam raised his hands in surrender, his heart pounding in his chest. The man in the suit spoke in a low, menacing voice, demanding to know why they were there.

 Sam explained their purpose, hoping to diffuse the situation. The man listened intently before finally lowering his gun and allowing them inside. The group breathed a collective sigh of relief as they stepped into the dimly lit foyer, grateful to have made it past the first hurdle. But they knew there were many more obstacles to come.

Vanlo, quick in action, came in front and said, 'Where is Zoyan? I need to see him on the front wall, which was covered with a huge portrait moved down to the floor of the room.' The man in the suit nodded and led them down a long hallway, past several closed doors.

As they walked, Sam couldn't help but feel a sense of unease. They were in unfamiliar territory, surrounded by people they didn't know, and they had no idea what they were getting themselves into.

 But they had a job to do, and they were determined to see it through. Finally, they reached a set of double doors at the end of the hallway. The man in the suit pushed the door open.

Sitting on a huge white king chair, smoking a cigar, with two beautiful but dangerous girls on both sides. Seated Zoyan Sam's heart raced as they entered the room. The atmosphere was tense, and they could feel the weight of the man's gaze on them.

They knew they had to tread carefully, but they were also confident in their abilities. Sam took a deep breath and stepped forward, ready to face whatever challenges lay ahead.

Vanlo pushed Sam to the side and gave him a look. Then he looked at Typhon and, pulling his muffler over his coat, swiped it on his right and pulled in an identical looking chair and sat on it with his legs crossing each other. Sam watched as Vanlo took charge, feeling a mixture of admiration and frustration.

He knew his boss was capable, but sometimes Vanlo's confidence could be overwhelming. As Typhon took his seat beside Vanlo, Sam took a step back and observed the situation.

He knew that they were in for a wild ride, but he was ready for whatever came their way. Together, they would face the challenges ahead and emerge victorious.

Vanlo just gave his right hand a jerk, and in front of him appeared a cigar. Pulling out the candle beside him, he also lit his cigar and took a deep puff, the smoke swirling around his head. Sam couldn't help but feel a twinge of annoyance at the smell, but he knew better than to say anything.

He had learned a long time ago that Vanlo was not one to be trifled with. With a nod from Vanlo, the meeting began, and Sam listened intently as they discussed their plans for the future. As the meeting drew to a close, Sam felt a sense of relief.

Suddenly, a gunshot was heard, and everyone started looking in all directions to know who had shot the Typhon. Vanlo quickly stood up, his cigar still in his mouth, and signalled for everyone to stay calm.

He slowly made his way towards the door, ready to face whatever danger lay ahead. Sam followed closely behind, his heart racing with fear.

As they stepped out into the hallway, they saw a figure running towards them, gun in hand. Vanlo quickly pulled out his own gun and fired a warning shot, causing the figures to stop in their tracks. It was then that they realized that the figure was actually a security guard who had accidentally fired his gun while cleaning it.

The situation was quickly diffused, but Sam couldn't shake off the feeling of terror that had gripped him. As they made their way back to their meeting, he couldn't help but think about how easily things could have gone wrong. He resolved to always be prepared for the unexpected, no matter how safe or secure he felt.

Sam looked at zoyan was pointing something at him over his left shoulder. Sam could not believe what he saw—he was bleeding. Vanlo had shot him and ruptured his ribcage, and the Typhon had come out of his left shoulder. Sam's thoughts were interrupted by the sudden realisation that his own safety measures had failed him.

He had not been prepared for this unexpected attack, and now he was paying the price. As he struggled to stay conscious, he knew that he would have to learn from this experience and take even greater precautions in the future. The incident had taught him that no matter how well-planned and secure a situation may seem, there is always the potential for danger around the corner, and he fell dead.

Sam's body hit the ground with a thud as zoyan stood over him, a look of satisfaction on his face. Sam's last thoughts were of regret for not being more vigilant and for underestimating the danger that Vanlo and zoyan posed. He had let his guard down, and now he was paying the ultimate price.

The lesson he had learned was harsh, but it was one that he would never forget. From now on, he will always be on the lookout for potential threats and will take every precaution to ensure his safety. As his vision faded and his consciousness slipped.

No one who was present understood why Vanlo had killed Sam. upon which Vanlo started laughing out loud and smoked his remaining cigar, revelling in the satisfaction of his twisted victory. Zoyan joined in, their laughter echoing through the empty alleyway as they walked away from the lifeless body of their victim. Sam's fate was sealed, but their own was far from certain.

They knew that their actions would not go unnoticed and that they would have to be careful in the days to come. But for now, they were free to enjoy the spoils of their triumph and revel in its power.

Sam was an undercover cop who had joined the Vanlo Gang to make proof so they could capture him and put him in jail for his crime. However, Vanlo and zoyan had caught onto his plan and decided to take matters into their own hands. With Sam now dead, they felt a sense of relief and satisfaction.

But they were also aware that their actions would have consequences. They would have to be cautious and watch their backs in the coming days. As for Sam, his mission had ended in tragedy, but his sacrifice had not been in vain. His death would serve as a reminder of the dangers that come with being an undercover cop.

Vanlo smoked his cigar and snapped his finger, looking at the bartender girl. The girl at once pulled out a large glass, filled it with ice, and poured in ninety ML of vodka and brought it to Vanlo. He then slapped his left hand's finger, and a beautiful girl walked near him.

Vanlo crossed his leg, bent a little towards his left side, and removed his 60 mm golden gun and kept it on the table.

Vanlo took a sip of his drink and looked at the beautiful girl standing next to him. 'What's your name?' he asked, taking another puff of his cigar.

'Lena,' she replied, smiling at him. 'You come here often?' Vanlo asked, leaning in closer to her. Lena shook her head. 'No, I'm just visiting from out of town.' she said. Vanlo nodded, taking another sip of his drink.

'Well, I'm glad you decided to come here tonight,' he said, flashing her a charming smile. 'Maybe we can have some good time at my place.'

Lena's smile faltered slightly at Vanlo's suggestion. She had been enjoying their conversation, but the idea of going back to his place made her uneasy. She quickly came up with an excuse. 'Actually, I should probably head back to my hotel soon. It's getting late,' she said, glancing at her watch.

Vanlo's smile didn't falter, but Lena could sense his disappointment. 'Well, maybe next time,' he said, finishing his drink.

 Lena nodded politely and stood up to leave. As she walked out of the bar, she couldn't see the site.

A black Mercedes drove into the hotel door. And the back door opened, and a tall, slim beauty walked out and hit Lena's head with the back of a gun, knocking her unconscious. She was away Lena's fate was now in the hands of her attacker when she woke up. Her vision was dim, but she could see smoke rings coming over, so she jumped up and sat down.

She was in for a huge surprise as she saw Vanlo in front of her, holding a cigar in his hand. Lena was shocked to see Vanlo standing in front of her. She didn't know what to expect next, but she knew that she had to be careful.

Lena's fate was now in the hands of Vanlo, and she had to figure out a way to escape from him.

When she looked at the front table to the left of her, she saw a golden gun, an iced vodka glass, and Vanlo smoking his cigar. He got up and told her, 'I don't like girls who say no to me.'

Lena's heart sank as she realized the gravity of the situation. She knew that she had to act fast if she wanted to survive. Lena gathered her courage and tried to reason with Vanlo, but he was not willing to listen. With no other option left, Lena made a run for it, grabbing the golden gun on her way out. She knew that her fate was now in her own hands, and she was ready to fight for her life. And she shot her first round. The 60-mm Typhon hit Vanlo in the chest, and he fell to the ground.

Instead of a normal blood flow from the wound of a person, the blood was flowing like a fountain. Seeing this, Lena was speechless. She had never seen anything like it before. Lena stood there in shock, staring at the lifeless body of Vanlo.

She couldn't believe what she had just done, but she knew that it was either him or her. Lena took a deep breath and composed herself, knowing that she had to leave the scene before anyone discovered what had happened. With the golden gun still in her hand, Lena wanted to disappear into the night.

There was a tornado that struck the window of the room, and a creepy face, half human, half animal, stood in front of Lena. However, Lena quickly thought that it was just her imagination playing tricks on her.

She shook her head and took a step back, trying to calm her nerves. She knew that she had to act fast and leave the place before anyone found out about what had happened. With a heavy heart, Lena turned around and started walking away, leaving behind the lifeless body and the memories of what had just occurred. She knew that she would have to live with the consequences of her actions for the rest of her life.

Before she could open the door and walk away, she heard a lizard-like or snake like sound and a tail rounding around her waist, pulling her back into the room. Lena's heart raced as she struggled to break free from the grip of the creature. She realized that her imagination was not playing tricks on her and that she was in real danger. With the golden gun still in her hand, she aimed it at the creature and pulled the trigger.

The sound of the gunshot echoed through the room as the creature fell to the ground, lifeless. Lena quickly ran towards the room door, knowing that she had to get as far as possible, but she was pulled back and through the bed, falling onto the floor on the other side.

She looked up to see a figure looming over her, and she knew that this nightmare was far from over.

Her heart pounded in her chest as she scrambled to her feet, her eyes scanning the room for anything she could use as a weapon. But as she looked around, she realized that she was completely unarmed.

The golden gun had fallen from her hand when she was pulled through the bed, and she had no idea where it had landed. Lena felt a surge of panic rising within her as the figure advanced towards her, its eyes glowing with an otherworldly light. She knew that she had to think fast if she wanted to survive this encounter.

She had her clothes ripped off, and she was naked. Standing against the wall near the bed, a large tongue licked her up and down, and then she woke up, realising it was all just a terrifying dream.

She took a deep breath, trying to calm her racing heart, and looked around the room, relieved to see that everything was as it should be. Lena knew that she needed to shake off the fear and get back to reality, but the memory of the nightmare lingered, haunting her thoughts. She resolved to be more careful in the future and to always keep a weapon close at hand.

With a final shiver, the next night, when she reached the hotel room and was taking a shower, the same thing happened to her, but this time it was not a dream. Lena realized that she was in real danger and had to act quickly to protect herself. She grabbed a nearby object and defended herself against the attacker, managing to escape with her life.

From that moment on, Lena knew that she could never let her guard down and would always be prepared for any situation that might arise.

But nature had some different plans for her. The next night, what was left undone was to be fulfilled. She was raped, and her body was left in a pool of blood.

This was a tragic and horrific event that Lena had to endure despite her efforts to protect herself. It serves as a reminder of the importance of being aware of our surroundings and taking the necessary precautions to ensure our safety. Our hearts go out to Lena and all those who have experienced similar trauma.

The next day, when the police arrived on the scene, they were in shock after seeing the crime, as they had never seen this kind of crime scene in the history of their service. A few female police officers fell down due to fits, among many others who vomited on the spot

As they had never seen this kind of crime scene. The incident had a deep impact on the community, and people started demanding justice for Lena. The police launched a thorough investigation. Justice was not served, and the scars of the incident remained.

It is essential to create a safe environment for everyone and ensure that such incidents never happen again. We must stand together as a society and work towards creating a better and safer world for all.

Days passed, and nothing was done. The police were clueless and had no idea that, in this case, they were standing in the same place as day one pressure coming from all sides. The lack of progress in the investigation only added to the frustration and anger of the community.

It was clear that something needed to be done to hold those responsible accountable and prevent similar incidents from occurring in the future. The community continued to demand justice for Lena and pushed for changes to be made within the police department. It is important for law enforcement to take cases like this seriously and work diligently to solve them. Only then can we begin to create a safer and more just society for all.

One night in the disco, Vanlo was sitting and drinking his ninety ml vodka and smoking his cigar when he saw a slim girl dancing alone. He made his way over to her and started to dance with her. She seemed uncomfortable and tried to move away, but he persisted. Eventually, she managed to break free and run out of the club. Vanlo didn't think much of it and continued to drink and dance the night away.

However, what he didn't realise was that his actions had gone against the reptile king, and his thoughts and actions had consequences that he would soon face. He was heavily drunk, and when he came out, he saw a different girl near the valet parking, and his brain went zombie.

Lena's body was sent for a post-mortem, and the doctors who were to operate on her body were also horrified after examining the body.

This was never seen in a rape case where the body was broken so badly that the bones were crushed and half the blood of the body was not to be found. The police were quick to investigate the case, and they soon found out that Vanlo was the last person to be seen with Lena's before she went missing. They wanted to arrest him and charge him with rape and murder. Vanlo was shocked and denied all the allegations, as the evidence against him was not strong.

"Napoli, an ex-East Mafia don, is shot dead outside the hotel in Europe..." The events that unfolded after Vanlo's night of drinking and dancing had serious consequences, as he was accused of rape and murder. Despite denying the allegations, the evidence against him was not in his favour. Meanwhile, Napoli, an ex-East Mafia don, was shot dead outside a hotel in Europe."The police were baffled by the seemingly unrelated incidents", but Detective Maria Lopez had a hunch that there was more to the story than met the eye. She dug deeper into Vanlo's past and discovered a connection between him and Napoli, one that suggested a possible motive for the murder.

As she pieced together the evidence, Lopez realized that she was dealing with a complex web of lies and deceit and that the truth was far more sinister than anyone had imagined.

Now Maria has a plan in mind. She goes to her boss to request additional resources and support to pursue the investigation further. With her team by her side, she is determined to uncover the truth and bring justice to those who have been wronged. The case is far from over, but with Maria's dedication and expertise, she is confident that they will be able to solve the mystery and bring the perpetrators to justice.

Maria wants to enter the Vanlo gang and try to find out the truth about their involvement in the rape and murder cases, as well as their connection to Napoli's death. She knows that this is a risky move, but she believes that it is the only way to get to the bottom of the case. With the support of her team and the resources provided by her boss, Maria is ready to take on this dangerous mission and bring the truth to light.

The stakes are high, but Maria is determined to see justice served and put an end to the web of lies. She spends weeks researching and gathering information about the Vanlo gang, their members, and their operations. She studies their routines, their habits, and their patterns, trying to find any opening or opportunity to infiltrate their organization.

Finally, she finds a way in through one of their low-level members who is looking to defect. Maria meets with him in secret and convinces him to vouch for her and introduce her to the gang's leaders. She knows that this is just the beginning of a long and perilous journey, but she is ready to face whatever challenges come her way in order to uncover the truth.

'As she had just been brought in by the police squad from another country, she was not known to the crime world at large. This gave her an advantage, as she could move around unnoticed and gather information without arousing suspicion.' Maria knew that she had to be careful and stay one step ahead of the gang, as any mistake could put her life in danger. But with her determination, skills, and the support of her team, Maria was ready to take on this mission and bring the truth to light.

One night, a member of the gang called Maria and told her to come to the club as tonight Vanlo was to be there, and this was the right place for him to introduce her to Vanlo as Vanlo was a ladies man. After sunset, Maria knew that this was her chance to finally meet the leader of the gang and gather valuable information. She dressed in her best outfit and made her way to the club, her heart racing with anticipation and nerves. As she entered the club, she scanned the room for Vanlo and finally spotted him sitting at a table with his entourage.

She then scanned the room for the tipper member with a deep breath, Maria approached him. She tried to act natural and confident, hoping that her cover wouldn't be blown. The tipper member led her to Vanlo's table, and Maria introduced herself as a new member who was interested in joining the gang. Vanlo seemed interested in her, and they started talking. Maria tried to gather as much information as possible without raising any suspicions. After a while, she excused herself and left the club, feeling relieved that she had managed to pull it off.

When she was waiting for the cab, her eyes were introduced to a body bleeding in a blood bath, and there were a few policemen standing there near it. As she did not want her cover to blow up, she sat quietly in the cab and left the scene without attracting any attention. Maria knew that she had to report what she had seen to the authorities, but she also knew that she had to be careful not to reveal her true identity. She was determined to gather enough evidence to bring down the gang and put an end to their criminal activities. Maria knew that it would not be easy, but she was willing to take the risk to make the city a safer place for everyone.

The next morning, when she went into the office of her boss in disguise, her boss showed her a few photos from the crime scene, which took place last night. She was in a fix when she saw the photo, and it was the member of the gang who had introduced her to the club. Maria knew that she had to act fast and gather more evidence before the gang found out that she was working against them. She made a plan to infiltrate deeper into the gang and gain their trust to gather more information.

It was a risky move, but Maria was determined to bring justice to the victims and make the city a safer place.

Here, the boss informs her that the crime was not a normal murder, but it was a shock to the whole medical and police departments as the body had been ripped in a way that was not seen or heard of and that half the blood of the body had vanished Despite the shocking nature of the crime, Maria remained resolute in her mission to gather evidence and bring down the gang responsible. She knew that the stakes were high, but she was willing to take the risk to make a difference in her community. With a plan in place to infiltrate the gang and gain their trust, Maria was determined to uncover the truth and bring justice to the victims.

As she delved deeper into the gang's inner circle, Maria began to uncover more disturbing information about their activities. She learned that they were involved in everything from drug trafficking to human trafficking and that their reach extended far beyond the city limits. Maria knew that she had stumbled onto something big, something that could have far-reaching consequences for the entire region. But she was determined to see it through, no matter the cost. With each passing day, she became more convinced that her work was important and that it was making a real difference in the world.

 And so she soldiered on, driven by a fierce sense of purpose and a desire to bring about change. Even when she faced danger and setbacks, Maria refused to give up. She knew that she had a responsibility to the victims of the gang and to her community as a whole, and she was determined to see her mission through to the end. As she continued to gather evidence and build her case, Maria knew that the stakes were higher than ever before. But she also knew that she had the strength, the courage, and the determination to see it through, no matter what challenges lay ahead.

Maria Maria, come down, was a call out from a girl shouting from downstairs and Maria came in the balcony to check who was calling her name so loudly It was a young girl, Lucia, looking up at her with a mischievous grin on her face. Maria couldn't help but smile at her even as she felt a twinge of guilt for being so absorbed in her work that she had forgotten about the people around her.

'What's up, Lucia?' she called down, leaning over the balcony railing.

'Are you ready to go? I have a surprise for you!' Maria felt a surge of warmth in her chest as she looked again.

Lucia's excitement was contagious, and Maria couldn't wait to see what surprise she had in store. She quickly made her way down the stairs and over to where Lucia was waiting. 'Okay, spill it,' Maria said, grinning from ear to ear. 'What's the surprise?'

Lucia's grin widened even further as she reached into her backpack and pulled out a small, wrapped box. 'I made something for you,' she said, holding it out to Maria. 'Open it!' Maria eagerly tore off the wrapping paper, her heart racing with anticipation.

There were two guns and a few extra bullet magazines in the box. Maria took a step back and was frozen for a while. She couldn't believe what she was seeing. Her excitement turned into confusion and fear. 'What is this, Lucia?' she asked, her voice shaking. Lucia's smile faded as she realized her mistake. 'I'm sorry, Maria.'

'I thought you would like them. I didn't know you were uncomfortable with guns,' she said apologetically. Maria took a deep breath and tried to calm herself down. 'It's okay, Lucia. I appreciate the effort.'

But why guns? What am I going to do with them? Lucia said the boss had given a green signal for you, and now you are going to be a part of the gang, and your first assignment is on its way, wherein you need guns.

Maria's heart sank at the mention of being a part of a gang and needing guns for her first assignment. She had been hoping for a different kind of job, one that didn't involve violence or danger. But now it seemed like she had no choice but to go along with it. She thanked Lucia for the gift but couldn't shake the feeling of unease that settled in her stomach. She knew she had to be careful and make the right decisions to keep herself safe.

Lucia said, 'Pack your bags for a few days; I shall pick you up in the next four hours. We need to go for an important briefing despite her reservations.'

Maria knew she had to go along with Lucia's plan. She packed her bags quickly and tried to mentally prepare herself for what was to come.

She couldn't ignore the feeling of unease in her stomach, but she knew she had to be cautious and make smart decisions to stay safe. As she waited for Lucia to arrive, she couldn't help but wonder what kind of dangerous world she was getting herself into.

Maria had always been a cautious person, but she also knew that sometimes taking risks was necessary. She had never trusted Lucia, but she couldn't shake the feeling that something was off. She had a nagging suspicion that Lucia wasn't telling her everything. Maria took a deep breath and tried to push the doubts out of her mind. She reminded herself that she had made it this far by being careful and cautious, and she wasn't about to throw that all away now. As Lucia's car pulled up outside her house, Maria took one last look around her home, unsure if she would ever see it again.

She grabbed her bag and headed out the door, her heart pounding in her chest. As she got into the car, Lucia greeted her with a smile, but Maria couldn't help but feel like it was forced. She tried to push the thought away and focus on the task at hand. Lucia had promised her a job that would pay well and allow her to finally live comfortably.

Maria just had to trust that Lucia wouldn't lead her into danger. As they drove away from her home, Maria couldn't help but feel like she was leaving behind everything she knew and loved.

'Move! Move! There's nobody else!' The sudden urgency in Lucia's voice snapped Maria out of her thoughts, and she quickly shifted her focus to the road ahead. She took a deep breath and reminded herself that this was the opportunity she had been waiting for. With a determined look on her face, the person driving the car drove off into the unknown, ready to start a new chapter in her life.

Maria had always been one to play it safe, but she knew that in order to achieve her dreams, she had to take risks. As they drove further away from the city, Maria couldn't help but feel a sense of excitement mixed with fear. She had no idea what lay ahead, but she was ready for whatever came her way. Lucia had promised her a job in a new city, and Maria was determined to make the most of it. She knew that it wouldn't be easy, but she was willing to put in the work to make her dreams a reality.

As the car turned into the woods. The temporary camps were signs of a mass struggle. Maria couldn't help but feel a sense of empathy for the people living in those temporary camps. She knew what it was like to struggle and fight for a better life. With a deep breath, Maria closed her eyes and focused on the road ahead, ready to face whatever challenges were coming.

Lucia started a conversation and started asking Maria about her family. Maria smiled and was now in deep trouble as to what she should say or whether she should change the topic.Maria hesitated for a moment, unsure if she wanted to open up about her family. But then she decided to take a chance and share a little bit about her background. As they drove deeper into the woods, Maria tried to make up a story about her parents and siblings, their struggles and triumphs, and the lessons she had learned from them. Lucia listened intently.

Somehow Lucia's face expression was not very in tune with the story told to her by Maria, and she started feeling something was wrong. Maria noticed Lucia's reaction and immediately stopped talking.

She realized that she had shared too much and maybe even revealed some personal information that she should not have. Maria decided to change the topic and steer the conversation in a different direction. She felt relieved that she had taken a chance to open up, but she also learned that it's important to trust your instincts and only share what you're comfortable with. As they continued their drive, Maria and Lucia enjoyed the scenery and talked about other topics.

A giant of a man loomed in front, questioning them about their destination and their business on the road. Lucia quickly regained her composure and calmly explained their plans, while Maria felt a pang of fear in her chest. The man eventually let them pass, and they continued on their journey. Maria made a mental note to be more cautious in the future, but she was also grateful for Lucia's quick thinking.

They drove in silence for a few minutes, both lost in their own thoughts. Maria couldn't help but replay the encounter with the giant man in her mind, wondering what could have happened if Lucia hadn't handled the situation so well.

She also realized that she had been so focused on her own worries that she hadn't really asked Lucia what was going on. Maria decided to break the silence and ask Lucia.

Suddenly, Maria's eye saw two men standing on a watch tower in the middle of the jungle, and she thought about what was going on before she could think anything. She saw a well-suited man standing with an AK-47 in his hand, and on a closer look, she kind of recognised him as the wanted drug mafia man. Maria's heart began to race as she realized the danger they were in. She quickly turned to Lucia and urged her to turn the car around and leave the area immediately. Lucia, sensing the urgency in Maria's voice, did not question her and swiftly turned the car near the gate and drove in.

Maria did not understand; she thought her cover of being a cop was busted, and Lucia has brought her into the gang to get the true story as to what Maria is investigating about Lucia and her gang. However, as they drove away from the dangerous situation, Lucia explained to Maria that they were actually on a mission to take down the drug mafia man and his associates.

Lucia had been working with the police to bring them to justice, and she needed Maria's help to gather more evidence. Maria was relieved to hear this and felt grateful for Lucia's trust in her. They continued on their mission, working together to bring down the dangerous criminal organization.

They reached the place; it was a huge tent built in between the jungle, which was not known to the policy or army of that city. The tent was surrounded by armed guards. The car was parked a distance away, and both ladies made their way towards the tent. As they got closer, they could hear voices and see shadows moving inside the tent. Maria and Lucia exchanged a quick glance, silently communicating. Maria and Lucia go in through the front. They both nodded, and without a word, they set off on the side chair. Maria's heart was pounding in her chest as she looked at the right hand of Vanlo, Mr. Typhon. The most notorious mafia man wanted by the world.

Mr. Typhon sat with his hand resting on the table, a gun in plain sight next to him. Maria and Lucia took a deep breath and walked towards him, trying to remain calm and composed.

As they approached, Mr. Typhon looked up and studied them for a moment before nodding his head in acknowledgement. The tension in the room was palpable as Mr. Typhon was breaking a few bones of a person they had caught and were interrogating. Maria and Lucia tried not to let their fear show as they sat down.

Mr. Typhon's piercing gaze made Maria feel as though he could see right through her. She shifted uncomfortably in her seat, trying to maintain eye contact without appearing intimidated. Lucia, on the other hand, seemed unfazed by the presence of the notorious mafia boss. She sat calmly with her hands folded in her lap, her expression neutral. Maria couldn't help but admire her composure in such a tense situation. As Mr. Typhon continued his interrogation, Maria and Lucia waited patiently, unsure of what to expect next.

The sound of bones cracking echoed through the room, sending shivers down Maria's spine. She couldn't believe that this was the reality of the world she lived in. She had heard stories of Mr. Typhon's brutality, but experiencing it first hand was something entirely different.

She wondered what would happen if they didn't get the answers they were looking for. Would they be next in line for interrogation? The thought made her stomach turn. She looked over at Lucia, hoping to find some solace in her calm demeanour. But Lucia's eyes were fixed on Mr. Typhon.

The tension in the room was palpable, and Maria couldn't help but feel a sense of dread wash over her. She knew that they had to find the answers they were looking for, but at what cost? Would they be able to live with themselves if they resorted to the same tactics as Mr. Typhon? As the interrogation continued, Maria and Lucia remained silent, their minds racing with thoughts and fears. They could only hope that they would be able to escape this situation unscathed.

The person became unconscious. And Mr. Typhon bent back, looking straight through the eyes of Maria, and said, 'So she is the new girl you all want me to let here join the gang.'

Then, truncating sharply towards Lucia, he said, 'And who is this? Another spy?' Maria's heart sank as she realized the gravity of their situation. They were in deep trouble, and she didn't know if they would make it out alive.

She looked over at Lucia, and they shared a silent moment of understanding. They knew they had to stay strong and keep their wits about them if they wanted to survive. As Mr. Typhon continued his interrogation, Maria and Lucia braced themselves for whatever was to come next.

They had heard rumours about Mr. Typhon's gang and their brutal tactics, but they never thought they would find themselves in the middle of it all. Maria took a deep breath and tried to stay calm, but her mind was racing with fear and uncertainty. She couldn't help but wonder how they had ended up in this situation and what they could do to get out of it. As Mr. Typhon's questions became more intense, Maria and Lucia exchanged a worried glance, knowing that their fate was in his hands. They could only hope that they would find a way to escape before it was too late.

Mr. Typhon' lit his cigar, got up from the chair, walked towards Lucia, caught her, lifted her up, put her on his shoulder, and walked to the exit, smoking his cigar and laughing triumphantly. Maria stood frozen, not knowing what to do. She felt a mix of anger, fear, and helplessness.

 She knew she couldn't let Lucia go without a fight, but she also knew that Mr. Typhon was too powerful for them to take on alone. As he disappeared through the door with Lucia, Maria knew that their only chance was to come up with a plan and act quickly. She took a deep breath, gathered her thoughts, and started to think of what would come next.

Three black, tall, well-built, well suited men walked in with guns in their hands and called Maria to walk with them. They walked out, and they pushed Maria to move forward and took her to a tree. One of them moved ahead and kept his hand on the tree at a particular place, and in a second, there was an opening in the tree and stairs going down. Maria hesitated for a moment, but she knew that she had no choice but to follow them down the stairs. She took a deep breath and started to descend into the unknown. As she went further down, she could hear the sound of machinery and voices in the distance. She knew that this was going to be a dangerous mission, but she was determined to rescue Lucia and put an end to Mr.

Typhon's evil plans. With a newfound sense of determination, Maria continued down the stairs.

chapter 6

Back to First Love

But the North Tribal King had different plans in mind; he was a cruel and dangerous man to be believed and feared. Despite the warnings from his advisors, he continued to expand his territory and oppress neighbouring tribes. His thirst for power and control seemed insatiable, and many feared for their lives under his rule. It was a dark time for the region, and the future looked bleak as long as the North Tribal King remained in power.Many attempts were made to overthrow him, but all failed, and those who dared to oppose him were met with brutal consequences. The North Tribal King had a vast army at his disposal, and he was not afraid to use it to maintain his hold on the region. As time went on, the situation only grew worse, and the people began to lose hope. However, there was one person who refused to give up, one person who believed that there was still a chance to bring an end to the North Tribal King's tyranny. That person was a young warrior named Kaida.

Vanlo and his man were taken to the hills. These hills were very high, and only skilled climbers and brave men could walk them. The top claimants would change at any given time. This mountain of heavy danced frost, which had many stories, was a mythical place, just like the red mountains. Vanlo and his men were taken to the top to get advice on what could be done with these men from the chief adviser of the North Tribal King. Legends had heard rumours of this mountain and knew that it held secrets that could help anyone in their quest to overthrow the Kaida.

The North Tribal King once gathered a small group of loyal warriors and set out to climb the treacherous slopes, determined to uncover the secrets that lay at the top. As they climbed higher, the air grew colder and the wind stronger, but they refused to give up. Finally, after days of climbing, they reached and were greeted by an unexpected sight. A strange looking man was standing there holding a stick, which had a glob of light shooting now and then. The man only wore tiger skin around his waist and had a long beard that reached his waist. He introduced himself as the "Malayan" of this place. The North Tribal King also welcomed Malaya at the top of the mountain. Malaya shared his wisdom and knowledge with the king, giving them advice on how to defeat the Kaida.

Kaida, a skilled Mountain warrior who was once the owner of the power of this mountain, wants to overthrow everyone and rule over all. With his skills and magical powers, Kaida had gathered a group of like-minded individuals who were also fed on the same theory as the current situation. Together, they trained and planned, waiting for the right moment to strike. Malaya warned the North Tribal King that Kaida and his followers were a serious threat to their kingdom and advised them to prepare for an attack. The king, grateful for Malaya's guidance, promised to take action and protect his people.

As the sun began to set, Malaya bid farewell and disappeared into the darkness, leaving the North Tribal King with a newfound determination to defend his kingdom against Kaida's forces.

The North Tribal King listened intently to Malaya's advice, knowing that they needed all the help they could get to defeat Kaida and his followers. Malaya spoke of the importance of unity and strategy, and shared his own experiences in battling against similar foes. The king and his council took notes, eager to implement Malaya's suggestions into their own battle plans. As they discussed their next steps, they couldn't help but feel a sense of unease, knowing that Kaida and his followers were out there, and waiting for their chance to strike.

 But Malaya, knowingly or unknowingly, did not complete the truth about Kaida; the legends had said it in the past: due to a wrong move in the past, Kaida was cursed to never be able to harm anyone directly. And he and his men were submerged in this mountain. However, the North Tribal King and his council did not know about this curse and were unaware of how to find the power and use it in the king's favour. As Malaya disappeared into the darkness, the king and his council began to make plans against Kaida and his forces. They knew that the road ahead would be difficult, but they were determined to gain power.

The next morning, Malaya came in search of the North Tribal King and asked him to send out scouts to gather information on Kaida's movements while his army began the search and left in a different direction. Malaya had given them a few maps to work on to find what they were looking for. The North Tribal King agreed to Malaya's request and immediately sent out scouts to gather information on Kaida's movements. Meanwhile, his army began the search in different directions using the maps provided by Malaya. They knew that the road ahead would be difficult, but they were determined to find a way to use Kaida's curse to their advantage and gain power. With Malaya's help, they were one step closer to achieving their goal.

One of the groups hit a close entry, which was covered with rocks, and they managed to open it, but the opening was so deep and dark that no one dared to enter. They decided to send in a few of their most experienced scouts to investigate the opening and report back. The scouts descended into the darkness, their torches casting flickering shadows on the walls. As they reached the bottom, they discovered a narrow passage leading to a hidden chamber. Inside, they found ancient artefacts and scrolls that could hold the key to unlocking Kaida's curse. Excited by their discovery, the scouts hurried back to report their findings to the North Tribal King and Malaya. The road ahead may be difficult, but with this new information, they were determined to gain the power they sought...

Malaya ordered all the search parties to be called back and assemble near the opening that had just been discovered. They would need to plan their next move carefully and decide how to proceed with caution, knowing that their actions could have far-reaching consequences. But for now, they were filled with hope and anticipation, eager to uncover the secrets that lay hidden in the depths of the earth. As they waited for the rest of the team to arrive,

Malaya couldn't help but feel a sense of unease. He knew that they were not the only ones searching for the artefacts and that they would have to be careful not to attract unwanted attention. He also knew that the journey ahead would be fraught with danger and that they would have to be prepared for anything. But despite his reservations, Malaya was determined to see this through to the end. For the sake of breaking the curse and restoring the power in his favour.

Malaya knew the years that he had spent on this mountain and the kind of evil worship he had done for so many years. This was the time to test them. As he was thinking about what he needed to work on to understand the deep secret hidden in the depths of the opening, there was a huge thunderstorm hitting the mountains. The lightning was hitting a specific point again and again and causing unrest in the place.

Due to this unrest in the mountains, a couple of wild animals started to roam around the area, making it even more dangerous for Malaya and his team. But Malaya was not deterred; he knew that this was just another obstacle in his path to breaking the curse. He gathered his team and prepared them for the challenges that lay ahead.

There was a firelight around, and all the king's men were in it to protect them from the wild animals As always, Malaya was away, not to be seen , as he had gone ahead to scout the area and search for any clues that could lead him to the hidden secret. Despite the storm and the danger lurking in the mountains, Malaya was determined to succeed in his mission. He knew that the secret held the key to breaking the curse

For generations, many have been waiting to unfold the secret. The wind howled and the rain beat down relentlessly, with many eyes scanning the rocky terrain for any sign of the hidden entrance. For ages

Suddenly, a black panther jumped from the top of a tree in between the king's men and the king himself. Unaware of what to do, the panther got disturbed due to the smoke hitting the top of the tree. As the panther was annoyed, he started attacking everyone in his way. He created a hell for the men, who all tried to catch it, but in vain he destroyed everything that came in his way. The men were trying to get out of this trouble when a group of wild bulls raged their way through, destroying everything. Looking at this, the Black Panther jumped aside and made its way into the deep darkness, and the wild bulls had also passed away. But the damage was done on a huge scale; barring a handful of men of the king and the king himself, many were killed and plenty were severely injured. They had to go back down to their village to seek medical attention as nothing could have been done on the mountain top, so now the king and five of his best men stood, and the rest helped others back home. The five men dug a huge hole the whole night to bury the bodies of their dead warriors.

Malaya was not to be seen anywhere, and the king and the five men who had stayed back did not know what to do next, and they also did not have the correct location of the opening in the deepest mountain. The situation was dire, with many lives lost and injuries sustained. The Black Panther had caused chaos and destruction, and the arrival of the wild bulls only added to the devastation. Despite the efforts of the men, they were unable to catch the panther and prevent the tragedy. Now, the king and his remaining men were left with the task of burying the dead and figuring out their next move without the guidance of Malaya or knowledge of the mountain's opening.

The king and his men waited for months on the trail of Malaya, but they never returned. The king and his men were forced to return to their village with heavy hearts, mourning the loss of their fellow warriors and unsure of what the future held for their kingdom. The memory of the Black Panther and the wild bulls would haunt them for years to come, a reminder of the dangers that lurked in the mountains and the importance of being prepared for any situation. In the end, the tragic events that unfolded in the mountains had a lasting impact on the king and his people. The loss of their fellow warriors and the failure to capture the secret of the opening left them with a sense of uncertainty and vulnerability. However, the king never gave up his quest to look for the hidden powers. He knew that there were still many mysteries waiting to be uncovered in the mountains, and he was determined to find them. He spent years studying maps, consulting with other experts, and gathering information from travellers who had ventured into the mountains. Finally, after many long years of searching, the king discovered a clue that would lead him to the opening.

Years had passed, and one day the village outpost saw a dawn of dust flying fast towards their village. All of them thought that this was a kind of tornado that would destroy their village and kill all of them. But as the dust settled, the king and his army were shocked to see Malaya returning from the mountains. He had finally found the opening and the secret powers that lay within. The king greeted him and welcomed him to the king's room. There, the king and

Malaya spoke in Private for a long time.

The king was eager to hear about Malaya's findings and the secret powers that he had discovered. Malaya explained that the opening was hidden deep within the mountains and required a treacherous journey to reach. But he was amazed at what he saw. The secret powers were unlike anything he had ever witnessed before. Malaya went on to describe the incredible healing properties of the plants and minerals that grew in the area, but they couldn't be moved from there as the spirit that guarded them did not allow them as they were all under the command of Kaida. And till kaida was not out of the locked box the power is of no use to anyone. The king listened intently, fascinated by Malaya's discoveries. He knew that these secret powers could be of great benefit to his kingdom, but the mention of Kaida and the locked box piqued his curiosity even further. He asked Malaya to elaborate on this mysterious figure and the locked box. Malaya hesitated at first, unsure if he should reveal too much, but the king's insistence eventually convinced him to share what he knew. He explained that Kaida was a powerful sorcerer who had been locked away in a magical box by a group of ancient wizards. The box was said to be in the cave, which needs to be discovered yet.

Malaya said there were many life sacrifices to be made, and once the right human was found and his blood would be offered, Kaida would himself come in and show the box from which he needed to be freed The king was both intrigued and apprehensive about this information. He knew that the power of Kaida could be a valuable asset to his kingdom, but he was also aware of the dangers that came with unleashing such a powerful sorcerer. He thanked Malaya for his insights and promised to consider his words carefully before making any decisions.

The meeting went on for a very long time when suddenly one of the king's men entered and said, 'Sorry, my lord, but the feast is ready to start. All are waiting for your presence.' The king had ordered a great feast in honour of Malaya. He knew that the man had travelled a long way to bring him this information, and he wanted to show his appreciation. As they made their way to the place, the king couldn't help but wonder about the box that Malaya had mentioned. He had heard stories about Kaida and his powers, but he had never believed them to be true. Now he was starting to think that there might be some truth to them after all. He made a mental note to send some of his best men to search for the cave where the box was said to be hidden. If there was even a slim chance of getting it.

When the feast started, there were different types of meat, fruits, and bread to feast on. The ladies were dancing, drinking forest drinks, and smoking betel leaf pipes. The king joined in the festivities, enjoying the delicious food and the lively music. He couldn't help but feel grateful for the man who had brought him such valuable information. He knew that with the box in his possession, he would have an edge over his enemies. As the night wore on, the king made plans to send his best men on a quest to find the box. He was determined to get his hands on it, no matter what it took. With a sense of purpose, Malaya got up at night and said, 'Now I need to leave.'

He reminded the king of the human sacrifice that needs to be given, so the king needs to send the human on the mountain top to do the needful, and to get this done perfectly, he said he would send in one of his main men who would serve the king as the chief advisor. Here comes Chota Lilitu, the wicked little Ghost in human form.

The wizards had warned about Chota Lilitu, saying that he was a dangerous and unpredictable character. But Malaya was confident in his choice and left the festivities, ready to set his plans in motion. The king, eager to obtain the box, agreed to Malaya's proposal and tasked Chota Lilitu with the mission. Little did they know that Chota Lilitu had his own agenda and would stop at nothing to get what he wanted? The future of the kingdom hung in the balance as the quest for the box began.

Things started to change. It had been almost ten years, and in these years, no one could keep count of how many people were captured and sent to the mountains for sacrifice, but there was one more thing that was happening in the village: every six months, a young girl would disappear, never to be seen again. This was a terrifying reality for the villagers, and they lived in constant fear of losing their daughters to this unknown force. Despite their efforts to find the culprit, no one has been able to uncover the truth behind these disappearances. The village was shrouded in a cloud of mystery and fear, and the people could only hope and pray that their loved ones would be spared from this fate.The village elders had called for a meeting to discuss the issue and come up with a solution. They had invited a renowned investigator from the Heebobo tribe to help them in their search. The investigator arrived the next day, a tall, imposing figure with piercing blue eyes and a commanding presence. He listened carefully as the villagers narrated their stories, taking notes and asking questions. He promised to do everything in his power to solve the mystery and bring peace to the village. The villagers felt a glimmer of hope and gratitude towards the investigator, and they eagerly awaited his findings. The investigator spent several days gathering information and studying the patterns of the disappearances. He interviewed witnesses and scoured the surrounding areas for any clues or evidence. Finally, he called for another meeting with the village elders and presented his findings. The culprit, he revealed, was not a human but a pack of wild animals that had been attacking villagers who strayed too far from the village.

The villagers were shocked and relieved at the same time. They had feared a human monster, but the reality was something they could deal with. It was Chota, the ghost man, who was behind all the missing girls. He had been haunting the village for years, and the superstitions of the villagers had led them to believe that he was responsible for the disappearances. The investigator explained that Chota was just a myth and that the real threat had been the wild animals. The villagers were grateful for the investigator's work and vowed to take measures to protect themselves from future attacks. They also promised to spread the word about the true cause of the disappearances so that other villages wouldn't fall prey to the same misconceptions. The investigator left the village feeling satisfied that he had solved the mystery. But he did not know that Chota had created a magical kingdom inside a huge tree in the underworld.

No one knew that Kaida had chosen him to remove him from the magical box that had trapped him for centuries and that he was now free to wreak havoc on the living world. As the investigator drove away, Chota's sinister laughter echoed through the forest, signalling the beginning of a new reign of terror. Little did anyone know that the real nightmare was just beginning?

Chota would capture young girls and send them into the dark of the castle where the only screaming of the girls could be heard for some time, and then a drop of blood would come and hit the forehead of Chota, which would signal him that his job was done and that he had successfully added another victim to his collection. The investigator, unaware of this new threat, continued on his journey, leaving the village and its inhabitants behind. Little did he know that he would soon be drawn back to the village as the disappearances continued and the terror of Chota's reign grew stronger?

The true cause of the disappearances had been uncovered, but the danger was far from over. The investigator would need to return and face the dark magic of Chota.

The northern treble king, unaware of this, was very angry as his people had started to migrate to different places or get attached to nearby treble villages, causing a decline in his own tribe's population. He sent out scouts to investigate, but all in vain, as none could find out the right answer.

The king then thought that only Malaya would be able to answer his troubles, so he sent a few of his close men to bring Malaya to the village with all the royal treatment of a king. It seems that both Chota and the northern tribe king are facing their own troubles and challenges.

Chota's dark magic and reign of terror continue to threaten the village and its inhabitants, while the northern tribe king is struggling with a decline in his own tribe's population. The king believes that only Malaya can help him find a solution to his troubles, and he has sent his men to bring her to the village with royal treatment.

Malaya was at first reluctant to accept the invitation, saying he had a lot on his hands to complete and therefore would not be able to come down to their village; they needed to check some other way out.

However, upon hearing about the decline in the northern tribe's population, Malaya realises the gravity of the situation and decides to go to the village to help. It remains to be seen how Malaya will tackle the challenges posed by Chota's dark magic and the northern tribe's population decline. Little did Malaya know that the perpetrator or mastermind behind this was to be Chota?

As Malaya made his way to the village, he couldn't help but feel a sense of unease. He had heard stories about dark magic and knew that he would have to be careful when dealing with it. However, a solution to the king's troubles and helping the people of the village as he arrived, she was greeted with all the royal treatment of a king and was taken to the king's house to discuss the issues at hand. The king explained to him the severity of the situation and what the dark magic was causing.

Chota was also part of this discussion, and Malaya realized that he would have to confront the king in order to find a solution. It was a daunting task, but Malaya was determined to do whatever it took to protect his people and restore peace to the land. Because if he did not help now, his wish of completing the mystery of the mountain and getting the power would go to dust; hence, he came forward to help for his own selfish greed.

In the night, he asked the king for a quiet place where no one would come and a few materials for his meditation. The king agreed and provided Malaya with the necessary materials. Malaya spent the night meditating and trying to come up with a solution to the dark magic problem. He knew that he had to be careful and precise in his actions, as one wrong move could have disastrous consequences. The next morning, Malaya presented his plan to the king and Chota, and they all agreed that it was the best course of action. Malaya set out to gather the necessary ingredients and began to perform the work.

It would have been around three or four in the early morning when the clouds started to shine with thunderstorm lighting and started to hit strong lights on the earth's surface, illuminating the mountain and its surroundings. Malaya continued his work, undeterred by the storm, knowing that he was close to solving the mystery and gaining the power he desired. Finally, after hours of intense concentration and hard work, Malaya succeeded in breaking the dark magic spell. He was shocked to see the answer he got: a fast light hit the circle in which Malaya was sitting, and fire emerged. The sparks of the fire strayed around the fire, rising to 20 to 40 feet.

Malaya sat quite, knowing he had no option, and there was a huge blast, and there rose Chota from the fire, revelling himself in front of Malaya. Laughing loud and shouting, 'Have you got what you were seeking for? It's me, and I have been behind this for some time now. How are you going to?'

'Handle me now that you have uncovered my true identity?' Malaya was taken aback by the sudden appearance of Chota and his brazen attitude. Malaya had not expected the culprit to reveal himself so easily. Nevertheless, Malaya remained calm and composed, knowing that he couldn't fight Chota, as if he did so or even if he exposed him in front of the kings, his chances of gaining power would be over Malaya knew for sure that Chota had come here with his own plans, and why he came in as a servant was also a question mark Malaya knew very well that if he told the king about Chota. Chota, he would take no time in converting the village into a burning ground of hell and would then kill Malaya as well; hence, Malaya was taken back.However, he quickly regained his composure and decided to play along with Chota's game. He smiled and said, 'Well, well, well. Look who we have here. The great Chota, Chota himself. I must say, I am impressed by your boldness.' Malaya's words seemed to catch Chota off guard, and he looked at Malaya with a mix of surprise and suspicion.

'What do you mean?' he asked, his voice laced with suspicion. Malaya chuckled and said, 'I mean, you didn't have to reveal yourself so easily.' Chota raised an eyebrow, still unsure of Malaya's intentions. 'I'm not sure I follow,' he said cautiously. Malaya leaned in closer, his voice low and conspiratorial. 'You could have kept hiding in the shadows, manipulating things from behind the scenes. But instead, you came out into the open. Why?'

 Chota hesitated for a moment before answering. 'I wanted to see if you were trustworthy,' he admitted. 'And are you satisfied with what you've seen?' Malaya asked with a hint of challenge in his tone. Chota nodded slowly.'Yes, I am. You have shown yourself to be honourable and capable, and I believe that together we can accomplish great things'. Malaya smiled, feeling a sense of relief. He had been worried that Chota might have had ulterior motives for coming out in the open, but it seemed that his intentions were genuine. They had been working together for a few weeks now, and Malaya had already seen the benefits of having Chota as an ally.

With his help, they had been able to gather valuable information about their enemies and plan their next moves with greater precision.

Malaya went back to the king the next morning and told him that he had unravelled the mystery of the missing girls. He said that there was a veil in the stream that was doing all this, and now when he reached the mountain with the power of his master, he would pull out the veil. As of now, he has tied him to the secret chain. The king was pleased with Malaya's progress and thanked him for his efforts. He asked if Malaya needed any assistance, but Malaya assured him that he had everything under control. Malaya set out for the mountain,

On the other hand, Chota stopped vanishing girls from this tribe for some time, and he would go away without telling the king anything to a faraway land in search of young girls and bring them to the underworld.

One day, Chota was walking through the deep forest when, all of a sudden, a ball of light hit his back and fell ahead of him He turned around to see where the light had come from and saw a figure standing in the distance. As he got closer, he realized it was a young girl, no older than 10 years old. She had a determined look on her face and was holding a staff that glowed with the same light that had hit him. Chota was taken aback by the girl's power and wondered how she had acquired it. The girl introduced herself as Amara and explained that she was a witch from a nearby village. She had been watching Chota for some time and knew about his evil deeds.

He asked her why she was following him and why she had

focused the ball of light on him. Chota was surprised and a bit nervous that Amara knew about his past, listened as Amara explained that she had been sent by the Kukamari villagers to stop him from causing any more harm. She was engrossed in a battle with Chota, and both of them were determined to come out victorious.

Huge fireballs were seen running from right to left, up and down, and left to right. There were even huge thunderstorm blasts now and then, and they were so involved in the fight that Amara forgot that Tasha had come and stood behind her and placed a hand behind. Tasha introduce herself as the daughter of the clouds.

To be continued